A Festival of Ghosts

ALSO BY WILLIAM ALEXANDER

Goblin Secrets

Ghoulish Song

Ambassador

Nomad

A Properly Unhaunted Place

A Festival of Ghosts

William Alexander

Illustrated by
Kelly Murphy

MARGARET K. McELDERRY BOOKS
New York London Toronto Sydney New Delhi

MARGARET K. McELDERRY BOOKS
An imprint of Simon & Schuster Children's Publishing Division
1230 Avenue of the Americas, New York, New York 10020

MARGARET K. MCELDERRY BOOKS is a trademark of Simon & Schuster, Inc.
For information about special discounts for bulk purchases, please contact Simon & Schuster Special Sales at 1-866-506-1949 or business@simonandschuster.com.
The Simon & Schuster Speakers Bureau can bring authors to your live event. For more information or to book an event, contact the Simon & Schuster Speakers Bureau at 1-866-248-3049 or visit our website at www.simonspeakers.com.
Book design by Sonia Chaghatzbanian and Irene Metaxatos
The text for this book was set in Horley Old Style MT Std.
The illustrations for this book were rendered in pencil.
Manufactured in the United States of America
0718 FFG
First Edition
10 9 8 7 6 5 4 3 2 1
CIP data for this book is available from the Library of Congress.
ISBN 978-1-4814-6918-0 (hardcover)
ISBN 978-1-4814-6920-3 (eBook)

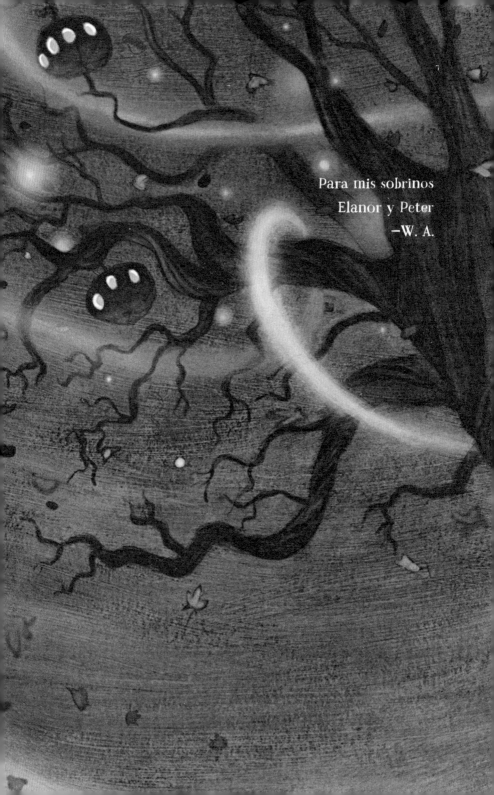

Para mis sobrinos
Elanor y Peter
—W. A.

A Festival of Ghosts

SEPTEMBER

1

ROSA CLIMBED A TREE IN THE HILLS ABOVE INGOT. She used one arm to climb. The other arm carried a pumpkin, which made her miss the next branch she aimed for. She lurched sideways, flailed, and caught a different branch. The pumpkin tried to roll out from under her arm, but Rosa didn't let that happen.

"You okay?" Jasper asked from the other side of the tree. They climbed opposite sides to keep from dropping pumpkins on each other.

"Yeah," Rosa said, "I'm okay." The pumpkin wasn't too heavy. She had hollowed it out and carved lantern windows into the sides. But it was still an awkward thing to haul up into a tree. She shifted her grip, reminded herself not to look down, and then looked down anyway.

Her heart grabbed both lungs to steady itself.

Rosa loathed heights. That never stopped her from climbing up and into high places, though. Her old library, back in the city, was full of massive wooden bookshelves. They towered like the trees that they used to be. And when Rosa had served there as the unofficial, too-young-to-be-hired-for-real assistant appeasement specialist, part of her job had been to climb all the way up to the tops of those shelves on tall, squeaky, wheeled ladders. They kept the wisp lanterns up there, and those lanterns needed tending, so Rosa had climbed. After tending to the lanterns she would sit at the very edge of a towering bookshelf and look down, even though the view would be nightmarish. Ghosts never gave her bad dreams, because she knew how to give those dreams right back. But Rosa often had nightmares about falling.

Her father used to comfort her after such dreams. "I've got you," he would say, over and over. "I've got you."

"Think this is far enough?" Jasper asked her.

"Nope," Rosa said, and climbed higher.

"We didn't spend this much effort yesterday," he pointed out.

"Somebody smashed all of our low-hanging lanterns yesterday," she answered. "These need to be way up high and out of reach."

"Did they break all the metal ones that Nell made?"

"Yes. They broke all the metal ones that Nell made."

"Rage," Jasper said. He said it calmly and quietly, as though reading a book to toddlers at the library. *This is a horse. This is a cow. These are ducklings. This is rage. Can you say "rage"?* Rosa wondered how to illustrate "rage" in a baby book. Show an adorable tantrum with steam shooting sideways from someone's ears? Or use a picture of a huge, erupting volcano with a face? That wouldn't be "rage," not as Rosa understood the word. To her it felt more like the molten and unerupting core of a planet. It kept the world in motion and alive. But it also scorched anything that got too close. Best to keep all that magma safely buried under miles and miles of solid rock.

"Rage," she cheerfully agreed.

"Oof," Jasper said as he climbed higher. "We should have rigged up a pulley system and hoisted these in buckets. Then we could've used both hands to climb, like sensible people."

"Good idea," Rosa said. "Let's try that tomorrow."

"School starts tomorrow," Jasper reminded her. "It does for me, anyway."

"Oh. Right." School was a strange concept to Rosa. She wasn't homeschooled, exactly. She had always lived in libraries, so she was *library*-schooled. Rosa read everything. She fell asleep each night to the rustling sounds of books sharing secrets with each other. She knew lots, and she knew how to look up things she didn't know—but only if those things interested her. She had no idea how to drum up interest for a topic that she didn't care about already.

Jasper pulled himself and his pumpkin up to a higher branch. Then he sat and dangled legs on either side. "I think this is plenty high. No one can reach us with baseball bats up here. Or broomsticks. Or even jousting lances."

Rosa agreed. She still lunged one-handed for one more tree branch and hauled herself up again, just to be sure.

Jasper tied his pumpkin lantern to a branch with a length of twine. Rosa did the same on her side of the tree. They both added candles, careful not to smudge the word carved into the wax: ἀλήθεια, or "aletheia." It meant "remembrance" in Greek. Sort of. Mom described aletheia as the world's memory of hidden things, but Rosa thought of it as a way to shout *Don't you DARE forget about this* to the wide and entire world. It also said *We remember* to all hidden things nearby.

Jasper lit his dangling lantern. Rosa leaned over to watch him, just to make sure he did it right. He did.

Then he put out his match by licking his fingertips and pressing them together.

She looked away quickly, pretending that she hadn't just kept tabs on his technique. Jasper learned fast—especially for someone who grew up *here*, in Ingot, a place that had been utterly unhaunted until very recently. But he was still learning.

Rosa lit her own match. The candle took the flame and kept it. Warm light bounced back and forth inside the pumpkin, absorbed and reflected by its yellow, damp, freshly carved walls. She whispered "Aletheia," and then licked her fingertips to put out the match.

Her foot slipped. Her heart lurched sideways. She dropped the still-lit match to catch herself. Then she watched it fall all the way down.

"Oops."

"What's wrong?" Jasper asked her.

I paid more attention to your lantern than mine, she thought.

"I might have just started a forest fire," she said out loud.

"That's bad."

"I agree." Rosa tried to figure out how to get down, which really should have been easier than climbing up but somehow wasn't.

A small, hard thing went whipping by her ear. She

heard a dull smack. Large pieces of pumpkin rained down on her head.

Rosa could think of several ghostly reasons why a wisp lantern might suddenly explode, and she mentally prepared herself to deal with one or all of those things. Such dealings would have been easier on the ground, where she could draw a protective circle around herself and not worry so much about falling, but she knew that she could probably still handle treed ghosts—or the ghosts of angry trees—from way up here if she needed to.

Is Jasper okay? she thought. *He looks okay. And his lantern hasn't exploded. That's good. So what happened to mine?* She looked up at the dangling wreckage.

Someone snickered.

She looked down.

Englebert Jones stood under the tree with a sling-shot in his hand. Humphrey and Bobbie Talcott stood behind him, their freckled faces glaring and impassive.

Bobbie crossed her arms. "Nice shot," she said.

Englebert took aim again. A small stone whacked the tree near Rosa's head.

"I wish I'd brought my sword," she said to Jasper. "It would have upset the wisps, so I left it at home. But a sword would be so useful now. *Speak to danger in its language, or offer it your own.*"

That was a quote from Catalina de Erauso, Rosa's

patron librarian and a great duelist of the sixteenth century. She killed so many of her enemies that she took up the arts of appeasement to calm their vengeful ghosts. Then she made a donkey-drawn cart into a traveling library and wandered the deserts of Spain.

"You probably shouldn't kill them," Jasper said. "Ms. Talcott is the mayor. She'd be upset if you slaughtered her children. And I can't imagine anything worse than to be haunted by Englebert Jones."

"I can," said Rosa. "It would be worse to be haunted by *me*."

She wondered what to do about this situation. Her match still smoldered down there somewhere. She could speak to it, and maybe coax it into a larger and more frightening flame. But that would be bad for the tree— and also bad for the two of them still stuck in the tree.

Englebert circled around, took aim with his slingshot, and shattered Jasper's lantern.

"Rage," Jasper said calmly. He took a pebble from his pocket and tossed it at the ground.

Englebert crouched, ready to duck and dodge, but the pebble landed far away from him.

"You missed," Bobbie said.

"I wasn't aiming for any of you," Jasper explained.

Rosa leaned back against the tree. *This should be fun.*

Other stones began to move. They rolled across the

forest floor and rose up from underneath it, shedding dirt and leaves to cluster around Jasper's tossed pebble. The stones gathered into the shape of a horse.

Jerónimo stood, reared up, and screamed. A living horse sounds terrifying when it screams, but the cry of a dead one is very much worse. Bobbie, Humphrey, and Englebert bolted for town. The haunted horse trotted over to the dropped slingshot, stepped on it, and broke it in half.

"Nicely done," Rosa said.

"Thanks," said Jasper. "My teacher should be proud."

"She is."

"I'm talking about your mom."

"Don't you talk about my mom."

They climbed down the tree. Jerónimo stood waiting for them. Rosa kept her distance—not because the horse was a ghost, but because he was a horse. Rosa was not a horse person. She busied herself by gathering up the two fallen candles and the match, just to make sure they didn't start a forest fire.

Jasper offered Jerónimo a sugar cube. Crushed sugar fell from the horse's stone-toothed mouth.

"I don't know if Ronnie can really taste anything," Jasper admitted, "but he does seem to *remember* the taste. Maybe that's enough."

"Ronnie?" Rosa had trouble reconciling the stone stallion with such an adorable nickname.

Jasper shrugged. "He isn't the same horse. Not really. He's a bit less and a bit more. So it felt weird to call him by his old name." The horse stamped a hoof. "And I think he expects a ride now that I've called him here."

"Go ahead," said Rosa. Jasper clearly wanted to ride, too.

"What about the lanterns?"

"We've got a few left. I'll just hang them from the lowest branches. They should be fine. For now. I don't think our pumpkin-smashers will work up the courage to come back tonight."

Jasper mounted up, which looked difficult. Jerónimo no longer tolerated saddles. "See you after school?"

"Right. School. Sure, I'll see you then."

The haunted horse cantered away with Jasper on his back.

Rosa watched them go. Then she watched Ingot. She could see most of the small town from here. It lay nestled in a valley like a shiny rock in the palm of a cupped hand. Late summer sunlight disappeared behind the western mountain range.

One by one, the wisps came out.

Dozens of small, floating lights flickered in the dusk like fireflies. They swirled through leaves and branches, lost and looking for somewhere to be.

Wisps had a reputation for pretending to be other

sorts of light—welcoming farmhouse windows, tail-lights on a mountain road, flashlights held by search parties—so they often got blamed for leading the living astray. That wasn't fair, though. It wasn't their fault. The wisps themselves were also lost.

Most of the ghosts in and around Ingot were still drifting, unsettled and unwelcome in town. But wandering spirits could use lanterns as rest stops and halfway houses, so Rosa gave them lanterns. This was good appeasement work. It made her mother proud. But that wasn't the only reason why she did it.

Rosa hurried to the wheelbarrow they had used to haul pumpkins uphill and into the forest. Four small, greenish, unbroken pumpkins remained. The pumpkin-smashers hadn't noticed them, apparently—or else they hadn't had time to smash them before Ronnie the stone horse chased them away. Rosa tied all four lanterns to one strong, low-hanging branch. Then she added candles.

"Aletheia," she whispered, because whispering was the proper way to speak with wisps. Loud noises upset them.

A floating light found a lantern and added to its glow. Rosa leaned in close.

"Is it you?" she asked, out loud but only barely. "Did you follow us here? Did you follow *her* here?"

The light faded, flickered, and then grew strong

again. Maybe that meant yes. Maybe it meant nothing.

"Mom was haunted by something before we came to Ingot," Rosa said. "She didn't like to talk about it. She still doesn't like to talk about it, even though she seems better now. But lots of things are looking for the places and the people that they used to haunt—or for the places and people that they would have haunted, if they'd ever had the chance before now. I can't keep them away. I wouldn't if I could. I won't banish you, either. But I'm still asking. Don't come looking for us. Don't haunt her."

The wisp flashed red before returning to the orange-yellow glow of candlelight and pumpkin.

"I'm serious, Dad," Rosa said, her voice louder than it should have been. "Stay away."

The wisp vanished. The candle flame went out.

Rosa felt stupid. "It probably wasn't even him." She took out the candle, poured drops of molten wax into the dirt, and then lit it with a new match to invite a new wisp.

Her stomach growled, long and low. Lunch was hours ago, and she was late for dinner. Rosa pushed the empty wheelbarrow homeward.

Thousands of wisps swirled around her as the evening sky darkened.

Larger, stranger things moved behind her, between the trees.

2

JASPER AND RONNIE RAN GALLOPING LAPS AROUND Ingot. They kept to the foothills, far from town and well away from anybody who might be shocked to see a boy riding a haunted horse.

"Whoa now," Jasper said after the third lap. "I think you're trying to tire yourself out. Stone doesn't get tired. But I do. My legs are cramping up. Shhhhhh. Whoa."

Ronnie clearly wanted to gallop like an avalanche. But he listened, and slowed.

They forded a river that came flowing down from the southern peaks. Ronnie lost some of himself midstream, but other, smoother stones gathered together on the far bank to replace the ones he had lost. They trotted out of the foothills and into the fairgrounds until they came to rest where they always did: right outside the locked gates of the Ingot Renaissance Festival.

Ronnie flared his nostrils as though breathing hard.

Jasper dismounted and stretched. "Ow."

The wood and plaster gates of the festival were all painted to look like big blocks of stone. Jasper had helped paint them. He'd been seven years old at the time, and he still remembered climbing the scaffold with bucket and brush.

A painted sign dangled above the gate. It read CLOSED FOR THE SEASON in medieval calligraphy, as though written by ancient librarians. A brand new chain and combination padlock held the gates shut. *I hope you're having fun pretending to be a castle*, the lock seemed to say, *but leave the real work to something shiny and chrome.*

Jasper twisted the lock tumblers until they read one-one-one-one. He had objected to the easy combination when his dad first installed the lock.

"It is the approximate birth year of Geoffrey of Monmouth the venerable librarian, chronicler of Arthurian legend and author of the *Prophetiae Merlini*," Sir Dad—Morris Chevalier—had answered with solemnity.

"Okay. Sure. But it's also just one digit repeated four times."

"Then it'll be easy to remember."

It was pretty easy to remember.

The lock clicked open. Jasper knew that he should not go inside. He went in anyway, and held the gate wide enough for Ronnie to follow.

The festival grounds smelled like dry dust and wet, rotting cloth. The place was also silent, and that was the strangest thing. It was *never* silent here—not in late summer, not even after closing time. Out-of-town performers always camped out on the grounds, and stayed up to all hours. Musicians wrote goofy new lyrics for old ballads and sang them after all the tourists left. Urchins ran around chasing fireflies and setting off fireworks.

"Urchins" was what everyone called the small children of festival performers and shopkeepers. Jasper had spent every summer of his life as one of those urchins, at least until he became old enough and horse-savvy enough to play a squire. His family had helped found the Ingot Renaissance Festival, the largest and most magnificent celebration of its kind to be found anywhere. His mother played the Queen. His father played Sir Morien, legendary Black Knight and unmatched champion of the royal joust. They had built this place, and at this time of year it was always, always loud.

Jasper moved cautiously across the quiet grounds. All of the shops, stalls, and theaters were shuttered up, bolted down, and only half repaired from the mayhem of two months ago.

Things went badly every time they tried to finish the repairs.

"We'll reopen next year," Dad promised several times daily. "We'll iron out all the new wrinkles by then."

One of those wrinkles took shape on the path ahead.

Dust swirled in a gust of wind. It pulled itself together, first in clumps and then into a long-limbed figure as thin as a pencil. The dusty, spindly thing took three steps across the path before falling apart. Then it pulled itself back together and took three more steps.

Jasper walked wide around it. Ronnie followed. His heavy stone hooves made deep prints in the dirt.

"Handisher!" Jasper called. "Where are you?"

Handisher was a tortoise, and unlikely to answer. The festival mascot wandered around in summertime with the queen's own livery draped over his shell. But no one had seen Handisher since the festival had closed.

Prop bins rattled against their own padlocks behind the Mousetrap Stage.

"They can hear us," Jasper said to Ronnie. "I think they want to come out and play. Even the practice swords play rough, though." He wished he'd brought his quarterstaff along, but Rosa had asked him not to. It might have upset the wisps.

The boy and his horse approached a mangled pile of cloth and wood that used to be the royal pavilion.

The pile stirred.

Strange shapes began to assemble themselves from the wreckage. They looked like puppets without puppeteers. Some were tiny, others huge and hooded. Several stood close together as though holding a private conversation.

Jasper watched them from a distance, cautious but curious. He needed to see this, all of it. He needed to understand the things that haunted his home, which used to be a completely unhaunted place. He needed to learn how to appease them.

Small ghosts began to glide above the wrecked pavilion on wings made out of sticks and scraps of cloth. One faltered, wobbled, and hit the ground near Jasper's feet.

He knelt beside the haunted thing, which didn't seem to be haunted anymore. It just lay there, inert. One of its wings had snapped. Jasper took twine from his pocket and tied the wing back together.

The glider stirred, flapped, and flew away.

Well that was satisfying, Jasper thought. *One small appeasement accomplished.* He glanced at the rest of the wrecked pavilion.

Every hooded thing had turned to look back at him.

Okay, he thought. *Time to go, then.*

Jasper scrambled up onto Ronnie's back. The horse tossed his head, clearly annoyed, but he trotted back toward the gates when Jasper asked him to with quick taps of his heels. Ronnie no longer tolerated reins.

A long row of ghosts stood on the roof of the Tacky Tavern. They wore canvas mining caps with carbide lamps attached, and swung their heads in unison. Bright beams of lamplight shone back and forth across the ground. Jasper wondered what they were searching for. He wondered if they were searching for him, and steered Ronnie well clear of the lights.

Gliding things circled above him on canvas wings.

"Hurry," Jasper whispered, and clicked his tongue. Ronnie hurried. Stone muscles strained against whatever ghostly sinews held them together.

They thundered down the path, avoided the rattling bins behind the Mousetrap, moved between shuttered shops in the market square, and finally burst through open gates. Nothing followed, either behind them or in the sky above.

Ronnie trotted back around. Jasper dismounted to lock up the gates. He didn't do this to keep the ghosts inside. They would not enjoy feeling trapped, and the little chrome padlock couldn't do much to hold them here anyway. Jasper locked the gates to keep the living out—especially those among the living named Englebert or Talcott. But those particular pumpkin-smashers were not the only ones who kept trying to pick fights with the dead. Best to keep everybody away from the fairgrounds.

It would probably be best to keep himself out, too, but Jasper kept coming back anyway. He still had a tortoise to find.

Ronnie nudged his shoulder with a pebbly nose.

"Goodnight," Jasper said. "I'll walk the rest of the way home. You would spook our living horses if you came anywhere near the farm."

Ronnie stamped a foot twice and then fell apart. A wide cairn settled where the horse used to be.

Jasper took one pebble from the pile and stuck it in his pocket.

3

ROSA DITCHED THE WHEELBARROW IN THE SHED
behind the library. She pushed it in too hard. The edge
dinged against a rusting motorcycle sidecar and rattled
all the copper scrap inside.

We need to get rid of that stuff, she thought. The
motorcycle, sidecar, and scrap had all belonged to Bartholomew Theosophras Barron, the founder of Ingot.
He had used copper to banish ghosts. But banishment
always backfired, and Barron's banishments had finally
backfired on him.

Rosa went around to the front entrance, which was
locked. Library hours were over for the day. But she
lived here, and this place knew who she was. The locks

inside the door clicked themselves open when they saw her coming.

Doorways are always haunted. Appeasement specialists are very good at moving through endings, beginnings, and haunted boundaries of every other sort.

She went inside and waved at the portrait of old Barron that looked out over the lobby. The musty air around her shifted from warm to cold and back as the ancestors of Ingot moved between shelves, looking for books that remembered them. Wisp lanterns dangled from the rafters.

Rosa walked slowly through the library, listening. One of the biographies made an unhappy noise about being misshelved. She put the book back where it needed to be. Three novels made gleeful noises about misshelving themselves on purpose. She put them back in their places.

"Excuse me?" said a small voice beside her.

Rosa looked, and saw no one. She blinked, looked again, and noticed the shape of a small boy suggested by dust motes drifting in the wisp light.

"Yes?" she asked quietly.

"I'm looking for a book," he told her. "I don't know what it's called. But it has a swimming dragon on the cover. And some jellyfish."

"I think I know that one." Rosa did know it. He

always asked for the same book. But she didn't know where to find it exactly, because the book kept moving. "Let's go look for it."

It wasn't on the shelf where it should have been. It wasn't stashed underneath that shelf, either, or tucked between the window sashes. Rosa finally found it behind one of the glass-eyed teddy bears that decorated the children's book section. She sat on the floor and read it aloud until she felt the dust motes of the boy settle themselves and drift comfortably down to the floor.

Her stomach growled.

"Shhhhh," she said to her stomach. "We're in a library."

"Roooooosaaaaaaaa!" Mom called from behind the audiobooks. "Is that you? Are you home?"

"Shhhhhhhhh!" Rosa shelved the bedtime story in its proper place, even though she knew it wouldn't stay there.

Mom found her. "Don't you dare shush me. I still outrank you in the Order of Librarians. Now hurry downstairs. Nell brought burgers, and yours is getting cold."

Rosa's stomach snarled again. She followed her mother downstairs.

Appeasement specialists always live inside their own libraries, or at least very close to their libraries.

They need to be on call at all hours. Some kinds of haunted disgruntlements only happen at night.

Rosa and Athena Díaz lived in a cozy basement apartment underneath the Ingot Public Library. Athena loved it, and said it felt like a fox burrow. Rosa was still getting used to living in a basement, but she did like the place better now that they had mostly unpacked. It felt, smelled, and sounded like all of their own familiar belongings. It also smelled like burgers.

"Hi Nell," Rosa said.

"Hi kid," Nell mumbled through a mouth half-full of burger. She was the town blacksmith. Nell made swords, spears, and armor for the Renaissance Festival—but that was before the festival shut down, unable to cope with the excessive number of revenants who haunted the fairgrounds. Now she mostly worked as a farrier. Nell made sure that horses stayed shod at the Chevalier farm. She also spent her time dismantling the huge circle of copper that Barron had built around the town to keep it an otherwise unhaunted place.

Her empty burger wrapper started to move across the kitchen table. The foil crinkled itself into a shape with legs. Nell's chair squeaked against the floor as she inched away.

Rosa tore into her own burger. She offered its wrapper to the thing that now haunted the tabletop.

It pounced on the extra foil and used it to make itself larger.

"Did you do that just to freak me out?" Nell asked pleasantly.

"Nope," Rosa said between large bites. "Are you still squeamish about ghosts?"

"Most locals are," Nell pointed out. "But no, I'm more squeamish about bugs. That foil-thing looks like a huge cockroach now. Do roaches ever haunt? Do I need to deal with the lasting grudge of every bug I've ever squished?"

"Probably not," Rosa said. "And if kitchen ghosts are bugging you, try grinding sage in your garbage disposal. Or rosemary, for remembrance. Either one."

"Thanks." Nell said. "I do *so* love hearing ghostly advice from the Díaz ladies."

Rosa smiled politely. "You're welcome." She started in on her fries, which were cold but still good and salty. Then she noticed more strange things piled onto the kitchen table. Notebooks. Binders. Number-two pencils. "Um, what's all this?"

Mom poured tea for the three of them and took a seat. "This is all for you."

Rosa felt suddenly unsettled. "I don't like pencils. Pencil sharpeners kind of freak me out. I like pens, and only if I've mixed up the ink myself, because then I can trust it to just write down what I meant to say. Remember that one red pen at the front desk of our old library? It hated vowels. You can't trust a pen that disemvowels all your words."

"You'll learn to use a pencil," Mom said.

Rosa looked at her mother, who sipped tea and looked back at her with a perfectly neutral expression. Rosa sent a pleading look at Nell. Nell only shrugged, clearly unwilling to interfere in Díaz family business. Rosa gave in and asked directly. "Why did you buy me school supplies?"

"Guess," Mom said.

"No. No, no, definitely nope." The greasy taste of cold fries turned unpleasant in her mouth. "You *can't* send me to school. I'm too busy. I need to make more lanterns. Ghost-hating vandals keep smashing mine."

Nell made a growly noise. "Even the ones that I made for you?"

"Yes," said Rosa. "Even the ones that you made. Completely wrecked."

The blacksmith cracked her knuckles. "Right. I'll make more."

"Thanks," Rosa said.

Mom set her mug on the table. The haunted foil-thing cautiously sniffed it. "It's time to take a break from the wisp lanterns, Rosa. You need to go to school."

"Don't make me go!" Rosa hated to hear pleading in her own voice. "I'll do *anything* else. Dishes. Bookbinding repairs. I'll deliver overdue notices personally."

"That's not a chore," Mom pointed out. "You enjoy it too much."

"Then I promise to hate it instead. Just please don't put me in a classroom!"

Mom gently nudged the foil-thing away from her mug. "Not all teachers are like Mr. Frumkin."

"What was he like?" Nell asked, curious.

"Mean," Rosa told her. "And he had haunted hair. I was just trying to help."

Mom sighed. "Rosa . . ."

"Is this about making friends?" Rosa asked. "I don't need any more friends. I've got Jasper. And I could probably find another friend if you really, really want me to. I'll start looking tomorrow."

"*Rosa.*" Mom used the voice that could make banshees shut up and listen. "This is not about you. Not exactly. You *should* learn how to talk to the living without scaring most of them away, but that's not why I'm sending you to school. It isn't just that you need to go. It's that the *school* needs *you*."

"That's ridiculous," Rosa said. "Why would they need . . . ? Oh."

"Yes," said Mom.

"Because the school is haunted now."

"Yes."

"Extremely haunted?"

"Yes."

"They don't already have a specialist on staff?" Rosa asked. "Not even in the school library? I guess not. They've never needed one before."

"And now they need you," Mom told her. "You'll go to class just like everyone else, but you will also be on call for emergency appeasements."

"Are emergency appeasements likely to happen?"

"Yes."

Rosa munched on the cold fries, which had become palatable again. "I'm starting to like this idea."

Mom sipped her tea. "I thought that you might."

"Will she get paid for this?" Nell asked.

"Shush," Mom said. "You're not helping. No, she won't get paid. She's too young to take the job officially. And the school can't afford to hire themselves a specialist on such short notice."

Rosa fiddled with a number-two pencil. "Won't you need me here, though? At the library?"

"Of course," Mom said. "Our first duty is to the library. But you do still live here. I'll squeak by during school hours somehow. The interlibrary loans will be the worst of it, but otherwise this place is in pretty decent shape—at least compared to the rest of town. Ingot used to be the least haunted place in the world. Now it might well be the *most* haunted place. That school needs you more than the library does."

Rosa didn't mind feeling indispensable. "Okay," she said. "I'll go."

"Thank you. Now off to bed. You'll need sleep for tomorrow. Don't worry about chores. I'll settle the rest of the library down tonight."

"Even the newspapers?" Rosa asked. "You usually hate dealing with the newspapers."

"Yes," Mom said.

"What do they do?" Nell asked. "Is it something that would freak me out?"

"Probably," Mom said.

"Then don't tell me about it. Night, kid."

"Goodnight, everybody." Rosa left them to their tea. The haunted foil waved.

Her bedroom was mostly unpacked. Her own books sat on their shelves, sorted by size and color rather than the strict fussiness of the alphabet and the Dewey Decimal System. Roland the toy penguin sat in the corner, quietly haunted by the ghost of a taxi driver also named Roland, next to a ukulele that Rosa's father had never learned how to play. Rosa didn't know how to play it either, but maybe she would someday.

She hung her tool belt on the wall next to her sword, which Nell had forged out of local copper.

Rosa wished she could bring the sword to school with her. *Better not*, she figured. *Local ghosts are practically allergic to this metal, and whatever haunts that place might take offense if I showed up heavily armed. The teachers probably wouldn't like it, either.*

She lit five of the six votive candles that she kept on the windowsill: four small white ones for her grandparents—who Rosa had never met or heard from, dead or living—and one big red one for her patron librarian Catalina de Erauso. Rosa had never met Patron Catalina, either, but ghosts that old and venerable tended to dissipate and did not usually answer the call of a candle.

"Recuerdo," she said, because her grandparents all spoke Spanish, and because Patron Catalina lived in Spain five hundred years ago. It felt wrong to say "remembrance" in any other language. "A todos os recuerdo. Por favor recuérdame." It also felt a little weird to promise that she would remember five people she'd never really known. But she did know their stories, and wished that they could know hers. She also wished she could speak more Spanish than just a few phrases. Even Mom's sense of the language seemed rusty now.

Her quilt started humming. Every patched piece knew a fragment of a different lullaby. All together it sounded like a discordant mess, but Rosa still found comfort in the noise. It reminded her of traffic, which she missed. Ingot was a much quieter place. From her basement bedroom she couldn't hear whatever small noises the town made anyway, because her window wasn't real. Someone had once tried to make up for the room's claustrophobic lack of windows by painting a landscape on the wall and then nailing a wooden frame around it. But the fake window did a pretty decent impression of the outside world. Maybe it remembered another view, from another place.

A sixth votive candle was marked with the name Ferdinand Díaz. Rosa lit it, but only briefly.

"Don't haunt us, Dad," she said. Then she licked her fingertips and pinched all of the flames away.

 **4**

THE CHEVALIER FAMILY FARMHOUSE HAD SPENT many decades settling its foundations into the ground, until it finally felt comfortable. Some of the walls and floors inside had shifted into odd angles. Jasper's own room was one of the oddest. It was large, but long and thin, with barely enough room for his bed at one end. The floorboards had warped into an obstacle course for Matchbox cars.

Jasper woke to the sound of stones scraping against that floor.

He leaned over the side of his bed and clicked on a flashlight.

Household spirits were moving their pebble pile again.

They do love small piles of pebbles, Rosa had told him. *Put a handful somewhere in your room to keep them occupied. It makes them feel welcome.* So he did. The spirits who haunted the underside of his bed had immediately stacked those stones into a small cairn. Every night they knocked it down and then slowly set it up again, pebble by pebble, in some other spot on the uneven floor.

It was almost time to get up, anyway. Jasper turned on the bedside light, which was made from an outdated globe that showed the nations of the world the way they weren't anymore. A poster of the solar system hung on the wall above the globe lamp. Next to that was a tapestry of a knight and a dragon settling their disagreements. On a shelf beside the tapestry sat a big pile of comic books and one framed photograph of Jasper's father, armored and on horseback, cradling his infant son in one arm.

Jasper climbed out of bed and out of his room. He brushed his teeth and set a coin on the new shelf by the bathroom mirror, just to say thanks and hello to anything that might be lurking on the flip side. Then he got dressed for his first day of fifth grade. The clothes were new. Jasper had grown a fair bit since the last day of fourth grade. Most of those clothes didn't fit anymore.

He paused to take up his quarterstaff, feel the

weight of it, and wish that he could bring it to school with him. The staff was useful for insisting on distance between himself and dangerous things. He knew that he definitely should not go armed to school, though. The rules of the festival didn't apply to the rest of the world.

He stuck the staff back into the umbrella stand, which was already full of wooden toy swords that Jasper had swung around as a toddler, and then went downstairs. The back staircase that led to the kitchen was narrow and awkward, as though built during a bygone age of very thin people. Jasper himself was fairly skinny, but his broad-shouldered father needed to turn himself sideways to take these stairs.

The Chevalier family kitchen was an anachronistic place. Centuries smacked into each other here. A shiny chrome fridge stood beside a fireplace large enough to roast a spitted boar (which they had never actually done, for lack of boar, but Dad very much wanted to try). A long table flanked by wooden benches took up most of the space. A merry band of mead-drinking warriors could feast comfortably at that table.

No one feasted at it now, but Jasper saw evidence that his father had eaten a quick breakfast already.

Unearthly howling came up from the sink. Jasper tossed some fresh rosemary down the drain to make it go away. "Shhhh," he said to the sink. "Mom's probably still asleep."

Jasper's mother taught history, or at least she usually did. This year she was taking a sabbatical. Mom planned to spend her time by writing a novel, repairing broken bits of the barn and stables, figuring out how to restore the Ingot Renaissance Festival to its former glory, and catching up on her sleep.

Jasper fixed himself some cereal and gobbled it down quickly. He went looking for his father and found him practicing fifteenth-century longsword techniques in the backyard, just like always.

Everyone has their morning rituals. We brush teeth and make sure that our socks match, or else make sure that they don't match in artfully pleasing ways. It gives shape to the day.

Sir Dad's ritual was to greet the dawn with a show of skilled swordsmanship. Sometimes Jasper joined him. This morning he very much needed to. Jasper wasn't sure what the first day of school would be like in a newly haunted Ingot, but he was sure that a practice bout would help him feel ready for whatever happened next.

He fetched two blunt training swords from the gardening shed.

Sir Dad set down his own blade, which was sharp-edged and therefore much too dangerous for fencing.

"Is that a new one?" Jasper asked.

Sir Dad nodded. "Nell just finished it. She's getting better at the decorative bits. Look at the family crest on the pommel, and the scrollwork at the base of the blade."

Jasper admired the decorative bits. "They look like copper."

"They are. Copper inlay over steel. It's local metal. I understand that this helps with ghostly disagreements."

"It does," Jasper said. "Try not to pick any fights, though. You can chase ghosts away, but they always come back."

Sir Dad smiled and swapped swords. "I'll be careful."

First they practiced master strikes, which had truly excellent names like "Zornhau." That meant "wrath-hew" in German. Then they took a few half-speed swings at each other. Sir Dad narrated the mock-fight as though describing it later, as a story told to an audience. "The knight struck with a Zwerchhau," he said, blade cutting high and sideways.

"The squire countered with another," Jasper said, parrying the first and striking back at the very same time.

The two got stuck trading that same move back and forth, both blades whirling overhead in a steady, ringing rhythm. This was Jasper's favorite thing to do while dueling with Sir Dad. He had named it "the whirligig" when he was seven years old. Then a band of festival musicians took up the name and called themselves Zwerchhau Whirligig. They specialized in mandolin covers of classic punk ballads. Jasper wondered where they were now. Probably on tour somewhere on the West Coast. Jasper hoped they would come back in the summer, when the festival reopened.

He hoped that the Fest would reopen.

"The knight yielded to the whirligig," said Sir Dad, savoring the silly word with a solemn voice. Then he broke the loop and stepped away.

Jasper put his training sword back in the shed. "The squire went to check on the horses. Then he went to school."

"Have a good first day." Sir Dad took up the new longsword again. It cut the air with a satisfying sound.

Jasper opened the sliding stable door and went in. The horses seemed skittish. They usually were these days.

Ronnie's old stall was empty. Mostly. A poltergeist had moved in. Jasper challenged it to a quick game of catch with the rubber ball that he kept there. Poltergeists love to play catch. They are much less likely to throw tantrums if they regularly get to throw a ball.

"Hey," said a voice that sounded like Rosa.

It turned out to be Rosa.

"Hey," Jasper said, surprised. "What's going on? More lantern trouble?"

"No," Rosa said. "I just don't want to walk to school alone. So I came here first. Even though it's in the opposite direction."

Jasper noticed her oversize backpack. "School? Really?"

"Yeah. Really." She shifted the weight of the backpack straps on her shoulders.

"You seem a little nervous," Jasper said.

"A little bit," she admitted.

"You weren't nervous when a stampeding tree tried to squish you."

"That was different," she said.

"Very."

"Shut up," she said.

Jasper grinned. "Wait here while I get my bag. It isn't nearly as massive as yours. What do you have in there?"

Rosa shrugged, or at least she tried, but her backpack was too heavy to let her shoulders move much. "A mix of school stuff and appeasement stuff," she said. "I might need more than I can fit in my tool belt. The building is very haunted, apparently."

"Yeah," Jasper said. "I've heard that, too."

He went inside to grab his own school stuff.

Rosa stayed put and waited. She didn't want to follow him into the farmhouse. It was always awkward to see Mr. and Mrs. Chevalier at home. *Hi! I'm so sorry that we messed up your festival. Well, I'm not completely sorry, because we all would have died horribly otherwise, but I am still kind of sorry.*

Fiore the horse snorted at her. She moved well away. Then she waved to the poltergeist on the ceiling. It waved back.

5

INGOT PUBLIC SCHOOL WAS A BIG BRICK BOX OF A place. It loomed. The windows looked like eyes, heavily lidded and uninterested in nonsense of any kind.

Dozens of other kids milled around outside the school, all calling out to each other and clumping into groups. Everybody seemed to know everybody else. Rosa missed the companionable distance of the city, and what it felt like to be surrounded by thousands of strangers all equally strange to each other. Rosa seemed to be the only stranger here. She shifted the weight of her massive backpack, surprised at just how much anxiousness prickled her skin.

Several other kids shouted Jasper's name. He waved.

"You know lots of people," Rosa noticed.

He shrugged. "It's a small town."

"I guess," she said. "I mean yes. It is. So where are we supposed to go now? I know my homeroom number, but I don't know which room that is. Or how to find it."

Jasper gave her a look. "You okay there, librarian? You can find books when they've deliberately hidden themselves inside the dust jackets of other books. I'm pretty sure that you can find a classroom."

Rosa breathed in slowly. "You're right. Okay. Let's go in." She headed for the entrance, but she didn't quite make it inside.

The front door broke through its splintering doorstop and slammed itself shut. Rosa stopped just in time to keep it from knocking her over.

"Interesting," she said to the door. "Are you really trying to keep me out, or just making some sort of point?" She tried the latch. It was locked. The lock wouldn't listen to her.

Jasper reached over and opened it easily.

"Interesting," Rosa said again.

"Still okay?" he asked.

"Oh, I am very much okay," she said.

"Because you've got that look."

"Which one?"

"The dangerous one."

"I like to think that I have more than one of those."
She clapped her hands and rubbed them together. It felt good to be dangerous.

She stepped over the threshold to see what might happen, but nothing else did. Then she glanced back outside.

Dozens of other kids stared at her through the open doorway. Rosa's sense of herself as dangerous slipped away in the glare of that attention. She couldn't hold on to the feeling, much as she wanted to. It was like trying to hug a wraith, and wraiths don't hug.

Jasper opened his mouth.

"Do not ask me if I'm okay," she said.

"Homeroom is over here," he said instead.

Worn wooden floors and freshly painted cinder-block walls made the school seem like an uncomfortable cross between a library and a hospital. The libraryish-ness should have made Rosa feel at home, but instead it felt more like an unsettling dream about home.

Once, back in the city, she had dreamed that a flood engulfed the central library. A mermaid who haunted the fountain outside came swimming right in and began to browse through biographies. She gave Rosa a wish-coin to eat. Rosa ate it and learned how to breathe underwater. This should have been amazing, but it wasn't. *Books don't like to get wet*, she kept thinking.

She couldn't remember *why* they don't like to get wet though, and the books wouldn't tell her. This bothered her until she woke up.

The mermaid later admitted that she had sent the dream on purpose, because she was bored. "You could have just told me how bored you were," Rosa had said. She dumped bucketfuls of old bath toys into the fountain for the mermaid's entertainment. It worked, mostly. The water spirit ate all the rubber ducks, but she spent weeks playing with the rest of the toys.

Most appeasement work was just a matter of figuring out what each disgruntled haunting really wanted.

Rosa wondered what sorts of things haunted this place, and what they might want.

"Welcome, students, to the first day of school," said a loud and disembodied voice over the intercom. "This is your principal speaking. I trust that you all had a wonderful summer!" The voice paused. "Please let your teachers know if you see or hear anything . . . weird. Um. Yes. Thank you."

"Was that supposed to be reassuring?" Rosa asked Jasper.

"Probably," he said.

"It didn't really work."

"Nope," he said.

Weirdnesses remained unseen and unheard for

the most of the morning, much to Rosa's disappoint-
ment. She spent the time sitting in a series of small,
uncomfortable chairs. Rosa listened to teachers, and
she listened to whispers that might have been ghosts
but turned out to be classmates having furtive conversations while they shot sideways glances at her. She
jumped, startled, whenever the bell told them all to
switch rooms. Minutes ticked by as though crawling on
their hands and knees.

I'm just a student, she said to herself, *just an ordinary
student, learning things about math and not waiting for
hauntings to start to make trouble, nope nope nope, definitely not.*

Things did get interesting in history class.

Rosa and Jasper sat next to each other.

"Noticed any weirdness yet?" he asked. Other students trickled in slowly and sat down—usually as far
away from Rosa as they could manage.

"Nope," she said. "Except for the fact that everyone
keeps staring at me."

Bobbie Talcott was staring at her right at that very
moment. Rosa stared back with the steady expression of
a duelist. Bobbie looked away first.

"They're just admiring your massive backpack,"
Jasper said.

"Shut up."

"Seriously. You could fit yourself in there."

"That's the plan," Rosa said. "This is a portal that will transport me somewhere very far away from here. All I have to do is crawl inside."

"Really?"

"No."

"Didn't think so."

"Yes, you did. For a moment there you absolutely did."

Rosa studied the classroom, looking for any sign of a disruptive haunting. The walls were covered with posters of famous writers and their famous quotes about history. Maya Angelou's poster smiled and insisted that *History, despite its wrenching pain, cannot be unlived, but if faced with courage need not be lived again.*

The teacher came in and dropped a heavy leather satchel on the desk.

Rosa stared at him.

He looked a whole lot like her dad.

"Hello, everyone," said the teacher. He wore glasses and a beard (unlike Rosa's father), walked with a limp and a silver-tipped cane (which was also unlike Rosa's father), and was clearly alive (which was very unlike Rosa's father). "My name is Mr. Lucius. I'll be your history teacher this year."

He wrote *Mr. Lucius* on the board. It was an old

slate chalkboard rather than a new, shiny, dry-erase whiteboard. The chalk made a squeaky rasp against the slate.

Mr. Lucius took attendance. "Jasper Chevalier."

"Here," Jasper said.

"Rosa Díaz."

It isn't him, she thought. *Definitely not. Mr. Lucius talks differently and walks differently, and also he's alive. This is normal. It happens all the time. People catch little glimpses of the dead in the faces of the living. Sometimes the dead are really there, hitching a ride and peeking out from behind a stranger's face. But usually not. Usually we're just trying too hard to see someone who isn't there, not at all, definitely not.*

"Rosa Díaz?" the teacher asked again.

Jasper kicked her foot.

"Here," she said.

"Are you sure?" Mr. Lucius asked, smiling.

"Not really," Rosa answered honestly.

But I am sure that my dad isn't here, she thought. *I'd know. If my father's ghost were in this room and haunting me then I would definitely know.*

"Isn't this supposed to be your Mom's class?" Rosa whispered to Jasper. She needed to think about someone else's parents rather than her own.

"Mom is on sabbatical," he explained.

"Do you ever call her 'Mom' while you're both at school?" Rosa asked. "Or do you have to call her 'Mrs. Chevalier'?"

"I have to call her 'Mrs. Chevalier.' And during the festival I always called her 'your grace,' or 'your majesty,' because she's royalty there. Here she's a teacher. And I'm a student. We've got roles to play."

Rosa wasn't sure about her own role. Was she really a student, or an undercover specialist pretending to be a student? What was the difference? If playing the role of an actual teacher was pretty much the same as playing the queen of the Renaissance Festival, then maybe there wasn't much difference between a real student and a pseudo-one. Rosa still felt out of place, as though misshelved and wearing the wrong dust jacket.

Mr. Lucius took up the chalkboard eraser and tried to scrub away the notes from a previous class.

All of those notes rewrote themselves.

He tried again. The notes returned. More writing followed until the board covered its whole surface in a swirling mass of chalk.

Rosa felt each moment of time fragment and separate from every other moment. The temperature dropped. She knew what that meant.

The chalkboard is remembering, she thought. *Every mark ever made on it is coming back. All the words, all*

the names, all the dates. All at once. The chalk looked like mist and fog swirling thick outside a window.

Faces pressed against that surface from the other side. Their mouths moved silently, shaping words without voices.

Mr. Lucius threw both arms around his face in a flailing panic. The eraser flew out of his hands and smacked hard against the chalkboard.

All of the faces vanished. The board emptied itself and became blank again. Chalk dust filled the room in billowing clouds.

The teacher coughed a couple of times. "Let's spend this class period at the school library instead of in here. Everyone go research something about ancient Rome. Anything about ancient Rome. Just go."

Students bolted from the room.

Unseen fingers tugged at Rosa's hair as she went with them.

The school library turned out to be a dinky little place with few bookshelves and several desks full of ancient beige computers. Rosa stood in the doorway, horrified.

"What's wrong?" Jasper asked her.

"This room and every single thing about it," Rosa told him. "But I guess it'll work as a sanctuary for our history class." She dug a pinch of salt from her tool belt and sprinkled it over the threshold. "Show me where to find the principal's office? I'm supposed to tell him about all the haunted things, so I should tell him about this. We can look for random trivia about Rome later."

6

PRINCIPAL AHMED SAT FIDGETING BEHIND HIS DESK. He clicked the button of his ballpoint pen several times. Then he wrote something on a pad of yellow paper and frowned at whatever it was that he had just written.

Rosa and Jasper stood awkwardly in his office doorway.

"Hello?" Rosa said.

The principal dropped his notepad. "Hello, students. Mr. Chevalier. And Miss . . . Díaz, is it? Yes? Hello. Come in. How can I help you?"

They came in and sat down.

"Something just happened in the history classroom," Rosa explained. "The chalkboard turned into a palimpsest."

"Excuse me?"

"Palimpsest," she said again. "Like an old wax writing tablet. You can rub them smooth, but traces of the old writing are still there. The tablet remembered everything ever written on it. The chalkboard just did the same thing."

"I know what a palimpsest is," said Principal Ahmed.

"Oh," said Rosa. "I thought maybe you didn't."

"I'm just surprised that *you* did. Quite the vocabulary word for a child your age."

"Hmm." Rosa bit back several things that she would have liked to say out loud. "I've always lived in libraries," she said instead. "Isn't my specialized oddness why you invited me to attend school this year?"

"Yes," the principal said. *Click click click* went the cap of his pen. "I suppose it is. Can you help us then? Make this stop?"

"No," Rosa said.

Click click click. "Really? I was told that you're an appeasement specialist. Practically a professional."

"That's true."

"But you are unwilling, or unable, to make this kind of disruption go away?"

"Both," Rosa said. "Unwilling and unable."

Principal Ahmed looked annoyed and bewildered.

Jasper tried to help. "Hauntings don't go away completely. There is no away."

"We used to enjoy a complete lack of ghosts here in Ingot," the principal pointed out wistfully.

"But they weren't gone," Jasper explained. "Just pushed off to the side. That can't last."

"Banishment never does," Rosa added. "I watched what happened after somebody tried to banish one lone poltergeist from a library. It brought the whole building down."

She had been sitting in a playground swing across the street, watching—just watching—while the Kasey Princell Memorial Library collapsed. Her father had been responsible for that place, but it turned out to be too much for him. Both of Rosa's parents had been inside when the trouble started. Only her mother made it out.

The principal stopped clicking his pen cap. "You're saying that it would potentially destroy our whole school to make the chalkboards usable."

Rosa shook her head, and tried to shake away the image of her dad's library as it collapsed in on itself. "No. I'm saying that we shouldn't try to unhaunt the classroom. But we should be able to appease whatever is in there and upset."

The principal put his pen down and clasped both hands tightly together. "What do you suggest, Miss Díaz?"

For one panicked moment Rosa couldn't think of any suggestions at all. *What am I doing here? What's my role supposed to be? Am I an appeasement specialist pretending to be a student, or am I a student pretending to be a specialist?*

"Treat the chalkboard like a mirror?" Jasper suggested.

Rosa nodded. "Yes. Good. Okay. You know how you're supposed to put coins and pebbles beneath a mirror?"

"Not really," the principal admitted.

"Oh," Rosa said. "Well you are. It's a way to show respect to anything that might be inside that mirror, and to ask permission to use it. If the teachers put coins on the eraser trays right before class, then ghosts inside the chalkboard will be more likely to share. A little salt sprinkled over the tray wouldn't hurt, either."

Principal Ahmed tried to take notes on his yellow pad of paper, but he gave up and threw the paper down. "Every time I write something, *anything*, it turns into a letter for someone named Beatrice. I don't know any Beatrice. And now there's a small blue flame hovering above my stapler."

He put his face in his hands and tried to breathe slowly.

Rosa nudged Jasper. She pointed at a decorative pile of very small pumpkins on the principal's desk. "Pass me one of those?"

Jasper handed her a little pumpkin.

Rosa took a pocketknife from her tool belt and began to carve into it.

Principal Ahmed looked up from his hands. "I'm going to have to confiscate that, Miss Díaz. We don't allow weapons at school."

"This is a tool, not a weapon." She pulled a small trash can closer to dump the pumpkin innards inside.

Jasper quietly groaned.

"The knife will not leave this room," Mr. Ahmed insisted.

"Okay," Rosa said. "It was cheap. I do go through a lot of them. Just let me finish this lantern—even though it isn't really a lantern so much as a small orange coaster to put a candle on. I think it'll work. Also, you should finish that letter."

"Excuse me?" he asked. "What letter?"

"The one to Beatrice." She searched the depths of her enormous backpack for a candle. "Finish writing it. Once that's done you'll probably be free to write other things." She found a candle all the way down in the bot-

tom of her backpack, set it inside the former pumpkin, and put both next to the stapler.

The blue flame moved to the candlewick. Its color shifted to a warm and steady orange.

The principal watched it burn. "Will I need to keep swapping in fresh candles?" he asked.

"Probably not," Rosa whispered. "This one looks like a wanderer to me. But here you go, just in case." She put another couple of candles on the desk, along with her pocketknife. He took away the knife and put it in a drawer.

I should go to Sir Agravain's store after school for another one, Rosa thought. *He'll probably let me put it on Mom's tab.* Sir Agravain's real, off-season name was Mr. Harrington. He ran the local hardware store. But at festival time he played a hapless knight who specialized in slapstick tumbles from the saddle. No one could fall off a horse as well as Sir Agravain.

"Thank you both," said Principal Ahmed. "I'll inform all the teachers that they should bring small coins and salt packets to school in order to keep their chalkboards calm."

He took up his notepad, took a deep breath, and tried to finish Beatrice's letter.

"You're welcome," Rosa said cheerfully. She felt better, like she finally knew what her role was supposed to be.

"It's lunchtime," Jasper said as they left the office. "Come on. I'll show you where to find the cafeteria."

Ominous shadows watched them from dark corners of the hall.

Rosa saw them and waved.

7

THE LUNCH ROOM WAS CLEARLY A GYM MOST OF the time, but foldable beige tables had turned it into a cafeteria. Basketball hoops had been winched up and out of the way. Four thick ropes hung down from one corner. Their dangling ends had been lashed together and looped over a hook on the wall.

"What are those for?" Rosa asked Jasper as they stood in line.

"Climbing up to the ceiling," he said.

"Why? What's up there?"

"You. Wondering why you're there. It's just something they make us do in gym class. Most kids don't climb all the way up to the top, though."

"Hmm." Rosa knew that she would force herself to climb all the way up to the top, even though she loathed heights. *Because* she loathed heights, really.

Right at that moment the ceiling looked like a nicer place to be than the floor. Rosa felt like everyone was still staring at her, even though they were doing the opposite. Every other student studiously looked away from her, their necks and shoulders tensed up from the effort.

The lunch line looped through the kitchen. Jasper pointed out what sorts of goop were likely to be tastier than others. They loaded up their plastic trays with the tastier goop.

A pocket of silence followed them around. Conversations withered at each table as they walked by.

Something whacked against the back of Rosa's head. She almost dropped her lunch.

Englebert Jones scrambled back to the table where Bobbie and Humphrey Talcott sat laughing.

Rosa felt something tug at her hair. She thought that it might be ghostly hands trying to catch her attention again. But it wasn't, not this time.

"He stuck a wad of green gum in your hair," Jasper told her.

"Hmm." Rosa poked at the gum. Then she smiled at her enemies. The smile made them uncomfortable enough to stop laughing and turn away.

"Let's eat outside," Jasper suggested.

"Can we do that?"

"Sure."

"Okay, then."

Rosa sheathed her challenging smile and followed him outside.

The two picnic tables were already full of teachers. Students sat in clumps on the ground, most of them near the hopscotch and foursquare courts painted in fading yellow lines.

Jasper led the way to the back of the playground, where a gnarled tree sat perched on top of a small, round hill.

"This is the Lump," he said when they reached the hill. "It's good for very short sledding runs and King-of-the-Lump games, though the tree is the undisputed king."

Three other kids were eating their lunch beneath the King of the Lump. The twins, Tracey and Gladys-Marie, had dressed identically today, right down to the purple hair ties in their natural ponytails and the matching frames of their thick glasses, but Jasper could always tell them apart anyway. Tracey loved comedies. Gladys-Marie liked action movies, but considered them comedies. Tracey had a gift for forgiveness. Gladys-Marie preferred revenge. Jasper had paid dearly for the Tadpole Incident when they were all nine years old. Neither twin had ever liked the Renaissance Festival, but they had different reasons for that. Tracey considered it silly. Gladys-Marie thought it was much too serious.

Both twins were right in the middle of telling their friend Mike a ghost story from their summertime travels. This was how Jasper's friends usually spent the first few days of school—by telling them about ghosts they had seen in places more haunted than Ingot.

The tradition felt awkward to Jasper now that there weren't any places more haunted than Ingot.

Jasper and Rosa got welcoming waves as they sat down.

Rosa tried and failed to pry the gum out of her hair.

Neither twin paused in their storytelling.

"We saw *another* one at the big upstate amusement park," Gladys-Marie said. She took a bite of lunch. Tracey smoothly took up the story while her sister chewed.

"If you sit in just the right seat on the Ferris wheel then a ghost girl comes to sit with you. She either fell from that seat, or she jumped. Or she was pushed. No one knows."

Tracey took a bite of her own lunch, so Gladys-

Marie took up the telling. "I wanted to ask her how it happened. I was all set to ask, but once we were sitting there with her it just seemed tacky."

"She was right across from us, all tightly buttoned up with her hands clenched in her lap," said Tracey. "She looked at the view. She didn't look at us. She didn't seem to see us at all."

"And she didn't jump, or scream, or fall while we were watching," Gladys-Marie added.

"She just disappeared before we got to the ground," Tracey said.

"That was it."

"That's all that happened."

"It was weird."

"Whoa," said Mike. He tried to push his hair out of his eyes, but the blond locks fell right back into place. Mike's hair always tried to hide him, as though quietly embarrassed for things that Mike himself never noticed or thought to be ashamed of.

All three of them took shivering delight in just how unsatisfying that story was. The ghost girl's unfinished business went round and round that Ferris wheel, and they didn't know why. They wouldn't ever know why.

Jasper used to love hearing about that sort of thing. Now he had ghost stories of his own to share. Should he tell them about the half-lion who harassed festival mermaids? The stampeding tree who smashed its way through the royal joust, crushed a bunch of cars in the parking lot, and later turned out to be the Lady Isabelle? Should he try to describe the green-bleeding town founder who had maintained a copper wall between Ingot and all the rest of its ghosts?

He gave up and made introductions instead.

"Everybody, this is Rosa. She's new. Lives in the library. Rosa, this is Tracey and Gladys-Marie. Tracey is on the left, Gladys-Marie on the right. That one is Mike."

The twins' wide eyes widened further. Maybe they had heard of Rosa. Maybe they already knew who she was.

"Hi," Mike said. Then he jumped right into telling his own ghost story, even though his mouth was half-full of lunch goop. "I think my cat, Tootsie, is back. She died last year, but now I keep hearing her purr in the middle of the night like she's trying to sleep on the next pillow. But there's nothing there when I turn the lights on. Maybe I should set out some of her favorite treats. I still have a bag of them. Probably stale, but I bet she wouldn't mind."

"You shouldn't," said Tracey.

"Definitely not," said Gladys-Marie. "If you feed the dead then they won't ever leave you alone."

Rosa picked at the goop on her tray. "That's not true."

Silence covered the Lump.

"If your cat is sticking around," Rosa went on, "then she won't leave no matter what you do. So you might as well make her feel welcome. I bet she'd like a treat."

"Oh," Mike said. "Good. Maybe I . . . okay."

The twins shared one of those looks meant to be inscrutable to everyone and everything else. They *definitely* knew who Rosa was.

Jasper wished he'd picked a different place for lunch. He tried to think of something distracting to say. But then both twins scooted up closer to Rosa.

"There's gum in your hair," Gladys-Marie whispered.

"I know," said Rosa. "I can't get it out."

"Let me try." Tracey took a fork to the tangled gum. "Don't worry, I haven't used this for anything food-related."

Rosa shrugged. "That's okay. I've got Englebert spit in my hair already."

"Doesn't he work at the Chevalier farm and the festival?" Gladys-Marie asked.

"He used to," Jasper said. "We fired him."

Gladys-Marie suggested other possible avenues of

vengeance while her sister fought the gum wad with her fork. Rosa seemed to appreciate both, even though the fork was clearly tearing out some of her hair.

Jasper felt less guilty for choosing this spot. He finished his goop.

"Did you see any ghosts this summer?" Mike asked him.

"Yeah," Jasper said. "A few." He still didn't know where to start. "I'll tell you about it later."

Lunch ended. Recess passed. The bell rang. The green wad of gum maintained its stubborn grip in Rosa's hair.

"I'm sorry," Tracey said, admitting defeat.

"Don't be," Rosa said. "Thank you. I think you wounded it. I can finish it off when I get home."

They gathered up their trays and climbed down the Lump. Rosa walked slowly. She wasn't in any hurry to go back inside the school.

The cafeteria door let everyone else through before it slammed itself shut against Rosa, knocked the tray out of her hands, and clipped the side of her nose. Leftover goop splattered her shoes. Blood dripped on her shirt.

She gave the door her most dangerous look.

8

THE NURSE STUFFED SOME COTTON INTO ROSA'S nose to stop the bleeding. The front of her shirt was already badly stained.

"Did you know that you also have gum in your hair?" the nurse asked gently. Her own hair was bright red, and tied back even though it clearly didn't want to be. Several scarlet locks escaped from the scrunchie.

"Yes," Rosa said, "I know." The cotton swabs in her nostrils stretched her voice into a funny shape.

"Peanut butter would help," the nurse said. "Unless you're allergic."

"I'm not," Rosa said.

"Then try it when you get home. Rub peanut butter into the gum to loosen its grip."

Rosa laughed. It hurt her nose. "That sounds like some sort of weird ritual."

The nurse also laughed, but nervously. "That's funny. Especially coming from you."

"So you know who I am."

"Everyone knows who you are, Miss Díaz. And you can go back to class now. Your nose isn't broken, but it will feel sore for a day or two."

"Okay," Rosa said. "Thanks. Also, you should probably keep your window open."

The nurse tugged at her hair scrunchie. "Why is that?"

"Kids come here when they're hurt," Rosa explained. "Over and over again. So all of that hurt is probably still here. It would be good to let some of it out."

"I see," the nurse said. "Thank you?"

"You're welcome."

Rosa left and eventually figured out which class she was supposed to be in.

Her fellow students spent extra effort to avoid her, alarmed by the scarlet stains on her shirt.

Teachers started to ask her what happened, recognized who she was, and then stopped wanting to know.

It was a long afternoon.

Rosa and Jasper walked home together, even though she told him not to. "Everyone is going to hate you just as much as they hate me. Go away. Save yourself. Leave me to sulk."

Jasper shrugged. "Too late. They've all seen us eat lunch together, so the damage is done. Lunch is important, you know. Most alliances are made and broken at lunchtime."

"No, I didn't know that," Rosa said. "I don't know anything about how the living draw circles around each other."

"You'll learn," Jasper promised. "There's another lesson following behind us."

"Oh really?" Rosa held up her phone and switched the screen around as if taking a selfie. She used the camera to glance back over her shoulder.

Bobbie and Humphrey trailed behind them along with their sidekick, Englebert.

Rosa put her phone away. "They seem to be unarmed. No slingshots, flamethrowers, ornate pole-arms, or gum. I still wish I had my sword."

"You still can't kill them," Jasper told her.

"But I can *hurt* them."

"Play nice," he said. "Remember that those two siblings are the mayor's own kids."

"Says the guy who sicced a haunted horse on them just yesterday."

"True," Jasper admitted. "But that was funny."

The library loomed ahead. It used to be a manor house, built by Bartholomew Barron to look like a small castle.

"Almost there," Rosa whispered. "Don't rush. Don't let them think they're chasing us inside."

"I wonder what they want," Jasper said.

"I can hear them running to catch up with us," Rosa said. "I guess we're about to find out."

She sat right down on the library steps and waited. Jasper sat with her.

Humphrey and Englebert paused, hung back, and tried to look tough about the way they kept their distance.

Bobbie Talcott came forward alone.

"Why are you doing this?" she demanded.

Rosa looked at Jasper. Jasper looked at Rosa. Both shrugged.

"Doing what, exactly?" Rosa asked.

Bobbie's scowl looked like it might silence songbirds and strangle their young. "The chalkboard freaked out today."

Rosa nodded. "I noticed that, too. But I'm still not sure why you think it's my fault."

"All of this is your fault!" Bobbie closed the gap between them and tried to loom over Rosa. "All of it. You control the ghosts."

Rosa shook her head. "I really don't."

"You can make them go back to wherever they came from."

"I really can't."

"Why won't you help us?" Bobbie demanded. "Isn't that your whole job?"

Rosa leaned forward and spoke very slowly. "I *am* helping. But they came from here. They belong here."

Bobbie took another step closer. "Who are you to say what belongs in this town and what doesn't?"

"I'm Rosa Ramona Díaz. I live here now. And you're Blanche Barbara Talcott, right?"

"Bobbie."

"Really? I heard that it's Blanche."

"Bobbie."

"You do know what 'blanche' means, right?"

"Yes. It means 'fair.'"

"It also means 'to turn sickly pale with fear and disgust.'"

Bobbie blanched. Then her face flushed the same color as her freckles. "The ghosts weren't here before you came to town. You brought them. I bet they'll leave if you do. They'll follow you out of Ingot if we force you to go."

"Nope," Rosa said. "Not how it works. I'd love to leave, but you wouldn't be any better off if I did."

Bobbie smiled. "We'll have to test that." She turned around and stalked away. The two boys fell in behind her.

"I think I kind of like her," Rosa said.

"She just threatened to run you out of town," Jasper pointed out. "What's to like, exactly?"

"She really thinks that I can command the dead," Rosa explained. "She thinks that graves open right up at my word. Wow. I'd be terrified of me if I thought that. But the fair Bobbie Talcott stood up and offered me a challenge anyway, so I guess I'm impressed. And flattered. I mean, she *is* wrong about pretty much everything, but her ignorance isn't my problem."

"It kinda is though," Jasper said. "She means to make it your problem."

"She can try." Rosa stood up, clapped her hands, and rubbed them together. "Are you coming over?"

Jasper shook his head. "I need to put in my daily search for Handisher."

"Need backup?" Rosa asked.

"Nope."

"Are you sure?"

"Yep. Thanks, though."

I don't think you're going to find that tortoise, Rosa's

expression said. *Even if you do, you're probably not going to like the shape that you find him in.*

"Good luck," she said out loud.

Jasper walked down Isabelle Road, toward the fairgrounds and home.

Rosa went inside. The smell of old and comfortable books welcomed her. Wisp lanterns winked as she walked underneath them.

Mrs. Jillynip sat behind the front desk and kept silent order with the force of her eyebrows. Rosa waved hello. The older librarian looked askance at Rosa's bloody shirt, but she didn't ask questions. Rosa didn't volunteer any answers.

She found her mother sorting small bottles of salt on the floor of their basement apartment. Appeasement specialists have many uses for salt.

"Hello, little love," Mom said. "How was school?"

I may have seen a glimpse of Dad in a stranger's face, she thought, but did not say. *He might be haunting me. Is he haunting you?*

"The school drew first blood," Rosa told her instead. "But I think I can handle it."

Mom looked up. "Ouch. Are you okay?"

"I'm okay. Do we have any peanut butter?"

"I don't think so," Mom said. "Never liked the stuff. Why?"

"Never mind."

Rosa went to her room, shut the door, and took her sword down from the wall. Then she grabbed the knot of her gum-stuck hair and cut it off.

9

JASPER FOUND THE FESTIVAL GATES ALREADY unlocked. A whole team of carpenters came tumbling out with their power tools, clearly terrified. This did not bode well for the cleanup and repair efforts.

"What's going on?" Jasper asked. He recognized Geoff and Po among them. Both played royal guards in summertime.

"The pavilion's fixed," said Po.

"Good," Jasper said. "That is good, right?"

"We're not the ones who fixed it," Geoff explained while running away.

The carpenters all fled across the field.

Jasper went though the gates and dropped his

backpack, which was heavy. He didn't want to be burdened if something encouraged him to leave very quickly.

He found ghosts in mining caps still clustered near the Tacky Tavern, though they stood on the ground this time. Some swayed back and forth. Others turned in a circle, very slowly, as if dancing to music played at half speed. Jasper had gotten more and more comfortable with ghostly company lately, but this particular group made him want to bolt like a horse spooked by snakes. He forced himself to walk in a calm and measured way.

Something tortoise-shaped moved nearby.

"Handisher?" Jasper whispered as he crouched. "Is that you? No. It isn't. You're just a rock."

The rock raised itself up, hovered above the ground for seven seconds, and then thumped back down.

"Hi," Jasper said. "Were you ever a tortoise? You are roughly the right size and shape, but I can't tell what you used to be."

The rock stayed put. Jasper waited for it to stir again, but it didn't. He moved on and made his way toward the royal pavilion.

This was the heart of the festival, the place where it had all begun. Twenty years ago Jasper's dad and a few other reckless history buffs had taught themselves how to joust. Then, last summer, a stampeding tree had wrecked the pavilion completely. But now that wreckage had all disappeared. Every stick and scrap had pulled together to become something else.

A crowd of figures stood like scarecrows, tattered cloth wrapped around their wooden bones. They didn't seem to notice Jasper. Instead they watched the lists. A long stretch of packed dirt and sand had been swept level again.

Two scarecrow knights on scarecrow horses charged at each other.

They met, and clashed, and shattered. Scraps fluttered slowly to the ground.

The crowd moved their arms as though clapping, but they lacked hands to clap. Their applause made a soft rustling noise.

The broken knights and their steeds remade themselves, piece by piece and scrap by scrap. They took up their places, clashed, and shattered again. The crowd rustled with more soft applause.

One of the knights carried himself like Jasper's father. His steed of wood and cloth moved just like Fiore. The scarecrow horse shook her head the same way, and made the same little skip-step right before the joust began.

That makes no kind of sense, Jasper thought. *Dad is alive. So is Fiore. So what sorts of ghosts are these?*

"Ghosts of the living," Rosa told him.

She set her cell to speakerphone, put it on her bedside table, and went back to practicing sword drills. Cut high. Cut low. Parry high. Parry low.

Her head felt light without a ponytail's worth of hair weighing her down.

"Meaning what, exactly?" Jasper's buzzing phone voice asked.

"Meaning that the fairgrounds remember," she said. "Whatever important stuff happened in a very haunted place is always still happening. That's what makes theaters so haunted. Actors play the same role in the same place, over and over, and then the role sticks around after the show is done. I'm glad Mom is a librarian rather than a stage manager. Theatrical appeasements are more stressful. Anyway, that knight isn't really the ghost of your Dad."

"It's the ghost of Sir Morien," Jasper said. "Dad's festival character."

"Exactly."

"So the whole festival is still there. It's just happening without us."

"Seems like." Cut high. Cut low. Parry high. Parry low. "Do you think this'll make it easier or harder to reopen next summer?"

"Harder," Jasper said. "We can't clean up that mess

and rebuild if ghosts are using the mess to build themselves new bodies."

"We'll figure something out." Rosa paused to stretch out her sword arm. "I should probably go. I can smell dinner defrosting. Or maybe I'm smelling some other bygone meal. Smells don't always go away in a home without windows."

"All the important stuff that happened in your kitchen is still happening," said Jasper.

"Nothing important has ever happened in our kitchen," Rosa said. "See you tomorrow."

"See you."

The phone blurped as the call ended.

Rosa cut the air one more time. She very much wanted to keep her sword close at hand. But she still couldn't bring it to school, not if tiny pocketknives got confiscated there.

"My huge, awkward backpack isn't really a portal to another place," she mused aloud, "but maybe I can make one."

She shoved her bed across the floor. Four cairns of small, stacked pebbles stood where the bed used to be. Rosa whispered an apology to household spirits as she moved each distinct pile to a new resting place under her bookshelf. Then she drew a perfect circle on the floorboards with chalk and string.

Nothing is stronger than a circle, Catalina de Erauso wrote centuries ago. *Nothing more whole in itself, nothing freer in its motion, for the scholars say that motion is most perfect when it rotates around a central point.*

Rosa used a camping compass to find and mark all four cardinal directions on the circle. She set the sword inside with its hilt against the easternmost edge and the tip of the blade pointing west. "East is for beginnings," she said. "West is for endings. We don't start fights, but we do finish them."

She pushed her bed back into place to hide both the circle and the sword.

OCTOBER

10

RED AND YELLOW LEAVES GATHERED IN DRIFTS ON the sidewalk. Jasper kicked them as he walked, which made a crunchy, satisfying noise.

Carved pumpkins decorated roughly half of the doorsteps he passed by. Candles burned inside those pumpkins, even though it was morning on a sunny day.

The other half of the houses he passed had curtains drawn and windows shuttered like eyes squeezed tight, or like ears with fingers stuck in. *Lalalalala-laaaaaaaaaaa. I don't see any ghosts, I don't hear any ghosts, and ghosts are most definitely not welcome here, nope.*

Jasper shook his head at the ignorance of his

neighbors. *The pumpkins give wandering ghosts a place to rest and keep warm,* he thought. *They're much more likely to wander right into your house if you don't give them a lantern instead.*

Yesterday he had carved four pumpkins for every entrance to the farmhouse and the barn. His mother had helped with the carving. His father had helped set the huge pumpkins into place. But neither one of them had wanted to talk about why they were putting big candles inside orange gourds. Both parents had been reluctant to discuss haunted things lately. This was frustrating. Jasper wanted to ask them what they thought about the fairgrounds and the fact that the Ingot Renaissance Festival carried on without them. It continued to reenact all of its summertime celebrations, without living performers or a living audience, even though summer was over. Jasper still didn't know what would happen when summer returned.

His mother said optimistic things like, "We'll work it out somehow," and then changed the subject. His father kept finding other places to be, other sorts of work to do. And he no longer practiced swordplay in the morning. That worried Jasper more than anything else.

Rosa waited for him on the front steps of the Ingot Public Library. She sat next to several pumpkin lanterns, some newly carved and others already smashed. Humphrey, Bobbie, or Englebert must have come visiting with baseball bats last night. Or maybe other kids had done it—kids who lived in one of the houses with tightly shuttered windows.

Rosa seemed cheerful enough despite the pumpkin wreckage. She wore a dress over blue jeans and her tool belt over the dress. Her hair had grown out a little bit since she had hacked it all off with a sword.

"Hey," she said. "You seem grumpy."

"Hey," he said. "You don't seem grumpy enough. I need someone to share my ire."

"Can't help you there." She stood up and set out for school. "Today I am feeling unstoppable."

"Careful," Jasper said. "You're temping fate to prove you wrong. Aren't you worried about jinxing yourself?"

"Nope," Rosa said. "I don't see any jinxes nearby."

She started whistling.

Jasper kicked another leaf pile. "How can you be so cheerful? Most of the other students cross the hallway to avoid you."

"True," Rosa said.

"The girls' bathroom empties completely the moment you go in."

"I like my privacy," she said. "And it's much easier

to talk to people inside the mirrors if everyone else clears out first."

"Bobbie Talcott put out a rumor that you can give a person haunted hair by making eye contact."

"I know!" Rosa said. "I love that rumor. Her own lovely locks would be doomed if it were true."

"What would haunted hair be like?" Jasper wondered.

"It mostly acts like it's out in different weather," Rosa said. "Soaked on a sunny day. Windswept even when you're indoors with all the windows closed. That sort of thing. The hair gets stuck in another time and place. Kind of annoying, but not really a big deal. Except for Mr. Frumkin. He was my teacher the last time I tried to go to school. It didn't go well. His apartment building had burned years and years ago, and he had the same haircut as someone who died in that fire. The place remembered the hair."

"What happened?"

"I tried to help. It sort of worked. Once he was bald the building didn't think that he should be on fire anymore. Hauntings do settle down by themselves sometimes. The chemistry lab stopped making that horrible noise."

"True," Jasper allowed, "but the lights still flicker whenever Ms. Giliani tells a joke."

"The lunch lady loves us now that we coaxed The Thing from Behind the Cafeteria Refrigerator into a more suitable place."

"The food is still awful, though," Jasper complained.

"Fie on you, Sir Chevalier. Nell MacMinnigan could forge horseshoe nails out of your grumpiness, but I am enjoying my bubble of contentment and I'll thank you not to burst it. Good day." She meant to cheer him up, or at least annoy him out of his funk, but it didn't work. Archaic words and fake European accents were a festival thing. Reminders of the festival did not improve his cheer.

They approached the school. Jasper looked up and saw what waited for them there.

"Rosa . . . ," he said.

She stuck out her chin. "I said *good day.*"

"Rosa!" he insisted. "Look at the Lump."

She looked at the Lump.

A whirlwind surrounded the hill behind the playground. The King of the Lump had shed all scarlet leaves, but none of those leaves touched the ground. Each one remained aloft and spinning.

Rosa crossed the playground and stepped right up to the edge of that spiraling wind. She tried to stick her hand through it.

"No good," she said. "This is a strong circle. I can't break it. Can you?"

Jasper pushed with his own hand, even though it felt like a dumb idea that might possibly cost him his fingers.

Air thickened around those fingers and pushed right back.

"No good," he said.

"Something must be buried under that little hill," Rosa mused. "Something that wants to be left alone. I should look at the library's map collection after school, see if I can figure out what's down there."

"Meanwhile we'll need a new place to eat lunch," Jasper said.

"Do we *have* to use the cafeteria?" Rosa asked. "I hate the cafeteria. Even though the lunch lady loves us. I don't want to navigate through the treaties, alliances, and grudges between all the different tables."

"It's not that hard," Jasper said. "And it's getting too cold to eat outside anyway." He led the way to the front doors, where other kids poured out of school buses and gathered into clumps. They stared at the whirlwind. They stared at Rosa and Jasper. Then they stared at the ground and shared urgent whispers with each other.

"Not that hard for you, maybe," Rosa said. "You

grew up here. Plus you're ridiculously attentive to the living, and can tell at a glance which best friends aren't best friends anymore. Or which people started kissing over the weekend and don't want to tell anyone else about it."

"Like Lucy and Chetna?" Jasper asked.

"What?"

He nodded his chin in their direction. "Pretty sure they've just started kissing. But don't say anything. They don't know how to feel about it yet."

Rosa raised one eyebrow at him, inspired by Mrs. Jillynip's constant expressions of disbelief and disdain. "You're creepy. How can you possibly know that?"

He wasn't really sure how, so he thought about it for a bit before answering. "Because I'm a festival urchin. I'm *the* festival urchin, really. Other performers' kids came and went, but I was there all day, every day, every single summer of my life."

Rosa's eyebrow remained raised. "You learned how to read minds by spending lots of time in the middle of a pseudo-historical costume party?"

"No," he said. "I just got a sense of where other people were at. And what connected them. That's all we were doing, really. I mean, we *also* played with swords and sang ballads with terrible puns in them and pretended to be on another continent, a thousand years ago, while talking to tourists from the present day. But everybody works together, aware of each other. They have to be. Otherwise it all breaks down."

Jasper felt sadness creep back across his body like frostbite. *We'll fix it*, he insisted to himself. *We can still rebuild, repair, and reopen next year. Even though the grounds are so chaotically haunted that no one is willing to go back there but me.*

He shifted the focus of the conversation back to Rosa. "How can you always tell at a glance what's haunting what?"

Rosa shrugged. "It's obvious."

"Not to anyone else."

"Then I'm gifted and brilliant."

"Or you grew up with it. Same as me. You know the dead like I know the living."

"Yeah, well, the dead are more consistent."

Everyone else hurried inside, eager to get away from the uncanny whirlwind surrounding the Lump. They also knew to keep clear of Rosa whenever she approached the unwelcoming entrance.

Jasper went first. He braced himself against the open door. Rosa took a running start. The door pushed and strained against Jasper's shoulder, but he held it until after she made it through. Then he followed. The door slammed shut behind them in protest.

"Thank you kindly, Sir Chevalier," said Rosa.

He mock-bowed.

"It's fun to say 'Sir Chevalier,'" Rosa went on. "Like a tongue-twister. 'Sir Chevalier sighed with a somber countenance. Sir Chevalier sang silly songs on Saturday.'"

"Come on," Jasper said. "We're going to be late for homeroom."

11

THE HISTORY CLASSROOM REMAINED THE MOST
haunted place inside the haunted school of a very
haunted town.

Jasper knew that he needed to get to class early, just
in case something unsettling happened. But he was running late because the toilet water in the boys' bathroom
had started to boil and he needed to deal with that first.

Billowing steam filled up the whole bathroom.
Unseen fingers wrote messages on the mirrors. Jasper
tried to read what they wrote, but all of the letters
dripped into an illegible smudge.

He flushed a pinch of salt down every toilet, which
calmed them down and stopped the boiling. The mir-

rors remained unreadable, so Jasper rushed to class. Air in the hallway felt brisk and chilly compared to the sauna that the bathroom had turned into.

Six students stood in line for the water fountain right outside the history classroom. Mike and Tracey were two of them. Mike waved, and then took his turn drinking.

"You're all flushed," Tracey said to Jasper. "Slow down. Looks like you ran a marathon to get here."

He couldn't help but laugh when she said "flushed." "Things got weird in the bathroom."

Tracey held up one hand. "Do *not* overshare."

"It was gross," he said. "Unspeakably gross."

"I'm not listening to yooooooooooou," Tracey sang loudly as she filled her plastic water bottle.

Jasper grinned and went in.

Most of the desks were taken already. Gladys-Marie sat in the back and kept the desk next to her reserved for her twin. Rosa sat in the front with emptiness to either side. Chairs close to Rosa always filled up last. She pretended not to notice this. Instead she looked up at the posters of history quotes. Virginia Hamilton declared, *The past moves me and with me, although I remove myself from it.*

Something tugged at Rosa's hair, even though it was short. She glanced back to make sure that nobody living was messing with her. Nobody was.

Jasper sat down next to Rosa.

"Your face is all sweaty," she said.

"Toilets started boiling in the bathroom," he told her. "Fixed it with salt."

"Good thinking."

"I know it was."

The last of the students trickled inside. Tracey sat next to her sister while taking a long sip from her water bottle.

Mr. Lucius came in and set his silver cane against the desk. "Good morning, everyone. Today we're going to talk about why the Roman emperor Aurelian was known as the Restorer of the World. Who can tell me one of his accomplishments?"

Rosa squirmed in her small chair. She knew a lot about history. But it made her classmates uncomfortable whenever she showed off just how much she knew, so she usually tried to keep a lid on her overflowing knowledge. Rosa also didn't like talking to Mr. Lucius, or catching his attention in any way whatsoever.

No one else spoke up. Awkward silence stretched across the room.

"Anyone?" the teacher said, still hopeful. "Come on. We went over this last week."

Bobbie Talcott raised her hand. Mr. Lucius called on her, clearly relieved.

"He built a really big wall," Bobbie said.

"Yes! Correct. He protected Rome by commissioning the great Aurelian wall. What else?"

"He burned the Library of Alexandria," Rosa muttered, just loud enough for Jasper to hear. Emperor Aurelian was not well loved among librarians.

Tracey raised her hand.

"Yes, Gladys-Marie?" Mr. Lucius asked.

He never could tell the twins apart. The real Gladys-Marie started to correct him, but then shrugged and gave up.

Tracey lowered her hand. She tried to answer. Silence followed. No words came out.

Everyone else started talking at once—or at least they tried. A few other kids silently panicked as they noticed their own voices missing.

Mr. Lucius clapped his hands together. "Quiet, please!" Then he looked embarrassed for having said that, because quietness was clearly the problem here.

"Take attendance," Jasper suggested. "Quick."

The teacher found the class list in his binder and called out names.

Six students could not say "here." Tracey, Mike, Chetna, River, Genevieve, and Lex had all lost their voices—or else those voices had been forcibly taken from them.

Mr. Lucius shut the binder and raised his own

voice in what was obviously supposed to be a firm and decisive way. This did not fool anyone. "Okay . . . okay. The six of you go to the nurse's office. The rest of us are going back to the library for another research assignment."

Gladys-Marie refused to leave her twin. She went with the silent six. "Someone who can still talk needs to tell the nurse what just happened."

"Right," said Mr. Lucius. "Okay. Good thinking. Everyone else, please follow me."

Rosa and Jasper did not follow him to the library. They went to find the principal instead.

Mr. Ahmed came with them to the history classroom, where they all lingered in the hallway outside. No one wanted to go back in.

"How soon can you sort this out, Miss Díaz?" the principal asked.

"Anywhere between minutes and months from now," Rosa said.

Mr. Ahmed made a noise between a grumble and a squeak.

"Whatever haunts this place must have something to say," she went on. "They wouldn't steal voices otherwise. We should listen."

They all moved a step closer to the open classroom door.

"I don't hear anything in there," the principal whispered.

"Me neither," said Rosa. *Think think think think think,* she thought. Then she took out a notebook and wrote all six names: Tracey, Mike, Chetna, River, Genevieve, and Lex. "Why did this happen to those six kids in particular? What else do they have in common? Are they all on the same sports team? Do their names spell out some sort of message?" Rosa, Jasper, and Mr. Ahmed stared at the names and silently rearranged their letters.

"Give, exert, carry keen evil achievement," Mr. Ahmed said. "That's one anagram. It sounds sinister, but otherwise makes no sense to me."

"Mix viler reek the teeny grievance cave?" Jasper suggested.

"I'm key revenge!" Rosa said. "Hear excretal invective."

Mr. Ahmed sighed. "This is both alarming and unhelpful." He went over to the water fountain and took a sip.

Something tickled at Jasper's memory. "All six kids were standing together right before class started. Right over there." He pointed at the fountain. "Tracey could still talk at the time."

The principal stood up slowly and tried to speak. He couldn't.

"Well, okay then," Rosa said. "That explains why it happened to those six in particular. Thanks, Mr. Ahmed. Maybe you should go to the nurse's office too?"

The distressed and silent principal left.

Rosa sat on the floor in the middle of the hallway. She turned to a new notebook page and filled it with every letter of the alphabet.

"More word games?" Jasper asked.

"Sort of," she said. "We should shut off this fountain before it steals more voices. But there's something I want to try first."

She ran the water over the fingers of her left hand.

"Shouldn't you wear gloves before doing that?" Jasper asked.

"Probably," Rosa agreed. "But I'm guessing that the water only takes your voice if you drink it. And I'm still talking, so I seem to be right."

She flicked wet fingers at the notebook page. Water droplets smacked into the paper.

"Talk to me," Rosa whispered to the water and whatever might be haunting it.

The letter T began to smear, followed by the A, L, C, and O. Then the T smudged again until it almost disappeared.

"Talcott," Jasper read.

"Interesting," Rosa said. "If it was Bobbie Talcott

you wanted, then your voice-theft just missed her. You hit six of her classmates instead."

She wrote out the alphabet on a new page and tried again. This time the P smeared first. R and O followed.

"Protect?" Jasper guessed. "That looks like 'protect.' But the T is so faded that I can't really tell. Might be 'project' instead. Or 'protract.'"

"Let's go with 'protect,'" Rosa said. "Does that mean they want to *defend* the Talcotts, or defend *against* them?"

She wrote the alphabet on a new page and tried again, but the soggy notebook refused to spell any more messages.

12

JASPER MADE AN OUT OF ORDER SIGN AND TAPED IT to the front of the fountain. Then he wrapped the whole spigot with a few layers of tape, just in case somebody ignored the sign.

"We should find Duncan and ask him to shut off the water properly."

"Duncan Barnstaple?" Rosa asked. "The festival candle maker?"

"That's the one," Jasper said. "He's also the maintenance guy here at school."

They both paused to look at the open classroom door.

"We have to go back in there, don't we?" Jasper asked.

"Yes," Rosa said.

"I'd rather not," he said.

"Likewise," she said.

They went inside the history classroom and shut the door behind them.

Every small hair on their arms stood up and suggested that they were not welcome.

"Feel that?" Jasper asked.

Rosa nodded. "At least it means that they've noticed us. They might listen. Might even talk now that they've got several voices to use."

She took up a piece of chalk and wrote *Hello* on the board in very large letters.

They waited. Nothing happened.

Rosa tried again. She wrote *Talcott who? What do you want with them?*

More nothing answered her from the other side of the chalkboard.

"Come on," she muttered. "Use the voices you took."

A dust bunny crawled out from underneath a shelf, took on the shape of an actual rabbit, and went loping across the floor before it dissolved back into dust, hair, and lint.

"That was Lafayette," Jasper explained. "Mom kept his hutch in that corner. He lived to be twelve, which is more than a century in rabbit years. And he seemed content right up to the end. I don't think he's the voice-stealing type."

"Hi Lafayette," Rosa said to the lint pile. "I'm glad you lived a good life. The hamsters that haunt our homeroom all died of fright."

"I hear Mr. Griffin plans to get another one," Jasper said.

"Really? Hasn't he accidentally slaughtered enough of them already?"

She continued to watch the chalkboard, which still did nothing.

"This might take a bit," she said. "Whatever haunts this place only just took those voices a few minutes ago, so they might not remember how to use them yet. We can wait. Which means skipping lunch. Are you okay with skipping lunch?"

"I'm very much okay with skipping lunch," Jasper said. "Especially now that we can't eat on the Lump."

"Hmm," said Rosa. "I'd forgotten about the Lump. Strange that it picked *today* to toss up a whirlwind circle around itself. So how is that hill and tree connected to a voice-confiscating water fountain?"

She put two candle stubs on the tray beneath the board, scratched ἀλήθεια into the side of a match with the tip of a pin, and used that match to light each wick.

"There," she said. "Hello. We're listening. Tell us what you need to say."

They waited, read books, and ate granola bars that Rosa kept in her huge backpack for just this sort of sudden, meal-skipping vigil.

Both candles burned all the way down to nothing.

Rosa made an impatient noise.

Jasper looked up from his book. "The school day is almost over."

"Yeah," Rosa said.

"So what happens now?"

"Now I plan to sulk. Eventually I'll ask Mom for help. She's probably too busy to help us out, though. A huge stack of interlibrary loans arrived yesterday. Extremely haunted books. Libraries in other cities haven't yet realized that they can't disinfect their most disruptive books by shipping them through Ingot. Not anymore. So Mom has her hands pretty full. She'll tell me that I should be able to figure this out myself. After that conversation I'll probably sulk some more." She cleaned up the two wax puddles and erased the unanswered questions from the chalkboard. "Maybe I could skip all of that and have dinner at your house instead?"

"I don't think my house will be any less tense," Jasper said. "I should tell Mom about the haunted things happening in her own classroom, which will make her unhappy. Then I'll ask Dad how the festival repairs are going, and he'll tell me that they're going nowhere because no one is brave enough to go in there for more than five minutes before they run away screaming. So I'd rather not head home yet, either."

"What should we do instead?" Rosa asked.

Jasper packed up his bag. "Let's go outside and glare at the Lump until we intimidate it into giving up its secrets."

"Sounds good."

They went outside, stood in the playground, and glared at the Lump.

It gave up none of its secrets.

"I wish we could break through this circle and take shovels to the hill," Rosa said. "I want to know what's buried underneath."

"I don't really wish that," Jasper said.

Rosa picked up a stick and tossed it at the Lump. The whirlwind took it and kept it aloft with all the spinning leaves.

School officially ended for the day. Other kids poured out of the building, avoided the playground, and hurried home.

"There goes Humphrey Talcott," Jasper noticed.

"Yeah . . . ," Rosa said thoughtfully.

"Think we should follow him?" he asked. "Try to

find out what his family name has to do with a haunted water fountain?"

"Yeah," Rosa said, so they followed him.

Humphrey kept checking his pocket watch as he walked. He loved that watch. He preferred Victorian history to the medieval and renaissance flavors of the festival.

"This feels weird," said Rosa. "Like we should be hiding behind trees instead of walking behind him, right out in the open."

"That would look a lot more suspicious," Jasper said. "We're just walking. Nothing weird about that."

Rosa whistled the sort of casual tune that people out walking might whistle to themselves.

They followed Humphrey as he hurried up a long, winding driveway to a huge house surrounded by manicured gardens.

"The Talcott household looks fancy," Rosa said. "Have you ever been there before?"

"Once or twice," said Jasper. "The mayor throws big midwinter parties. Mom hates them. Dad is better at the schmoozing. All of the important local business folk are expected to go, and my parents are the festival directors—the *only* directors now that Mr. Rathaus quit. Plus we run a big horse farm. So they go to the party, and sometimes bring me. It isn't fun."

Two landscapers dug a long, narrow trench at the base of the garden. Jasper recognized them both. "That's Geoff and Po. They play royal guards in the summer. And they promised to help with repairs, but then they got spooked." He waved. They waved back.

"What are you *doing?*" Rosa whispered. "I thought we were being sneaky."

"We are," he said. "Just act like we're supposed to be here."

"How?"

"Pretend you've got your sword with you."

She did. It helped.

They left the driveway to say hello to the ditch-diggers.

"Good day to you, noble squire!" said Po with forced cheerfulness. He stood next to a gardening cart covered up with a tarp, and he tugged on the tarp to make sure it stayed covered.

"And to yourselves," Jasper said. A slight echo of his festival character haunted his voice. "What are you working on?"

"An invisible dog fence," Geoff told him. "For the dog."

"Really?" Jasper asked.

"Yes," said Geoff. "Really."

"They don't have a dog," said Jasper.

"They're getting a dog," said Geoff.

"And we'd best get back to work," said Po. "The good mayor is a taskmaster. Taskmistress. Something like that. Goodbye."

"Farewell to you both," Jasper said.

The two kids trudged up the hill and toward the house.

"Well," Rosa said, "that was just a little bit suspicious."

"A bit," Jasper agreed. "Plus Humphrey's allergic to dogs. He could barely breathe at Mike's seventh birthday party, because Mike's family has several dogs."

"Interesting," Rosa said.

Cold rain began to fall on them. The ditch-diggers ran for their truck to wait it out. Rosa and Jasper took shelter on the front porch of the Talcott family home, which was massive and wrapped around most of the house. Thick white columns held up the porch roof. Rain struck that roof as though trying to punish it for something terrible.

"What now?" Rosa asked. "Knock on the door and say hi? We're not welcome here. We're not friends with anybody here. Bobbie keeps threatening me. Humphrey once fired a homemade flamethrower at you."

"Then he'll be very surprised to see us," Jasper

pointed out. "Maybe he'll drop his guard and say something useful."

"You're saying that I should try to look intimidating."

"Yes," said Jasper.

Rosa nodded once. "I can do that."

She knocked on the door.

Humphrey opened it.

13

HUMPHREY WAS AN EIGHTH GRADER, OLDER AND taller than either Rosa or Jasper, but he jumped as though they both towered over him in a menacing way.

"Hi," Rosa said.

"What . . . ?" Humphrey glanced down at the garden and then looked quickly away. "What are you . . . ?"

"We're just worried about you," Rosa said, her voice politely concerned. That sounded even more menacing, coming from her. "We've heard your family name in ghostly whispers."

Humphrey's eyes opened wide. "Come in."

Rosa glanced at Jasper. *Freaking him out seems to be working,* she thought.

Jasper shrugged. *We do outnumber him,* said the shrug. *He probably won't try anything violent.*

"Hurry up," Humphrey insisted. He waved them in and then shut the door quickly.

Rosa looked around. They stood in a foyer with a polished stone floor and a very large chandelier dangling above. A curved and theatrical staircase seemed made for greeting dozens of important guests with prepared speeches.

"Nice place," she said.

"What did you hear?" Humphrey's voice broke. He tried to clear it. "Were you standing close to Bobbie? Was something whispering behind her?"

Nope, Rosa thought. *Drops of water from a cursed drinking fountain spelled out your last name and we have no idea what that means.* But she didn't say any of that aloud.

"Whose voice is it?" Jasper asked without confirming or denying that they might already know.

Humphrey obviously wanted to tell them. He also looked hesitant and suspicious again. "If I tell you about it, you'll make it worse."

"Of course we won't," said Rosa. "Even if you deserve worse. My family business and calling is to make things *better* between the dead and the living."

"Things got much worse after you moved here," Humphrey said.

Rosa shook her head, exasperated. "You're mixing up causes and effects there, genius. Just because something happened *after* I moved here doesn't mean it happened *because* I moved here. If you get a perfect score on a quiz right after you get a haircut, that doesn't mean the haircut made you smarter."

Humphrey cranked up the scowling levels of sarcasm in his voice. "Right. Sure. Coincidence. But I saw Jasper break the circle that kept Ingot safe. And I know you were working together. He used a big candle and a weird ritual. He invited them all back inside. I was *there*. I saw him do it."

Jasper crossed his arms. "The circle was already broken. You were there when that happened, too. You saw me fix the breach and bring them home gently, before the wild flood of their homecoming killed everyone in town. *That* is what you saw. But you were shrieking like a terrified hamster at the time."

Humphrey looked like he wanted to slap Jasper with a glove and challenge him to a duel fought with ornate Victorian pistols. Rosa stepped between them.

"I'm bored," she said. "This argument bores me. If you want my help, then just tell me whose whispering voice you're so worried about."

"I can't," Humphrey said. "I can't say her name. She'll hear me. She'll know."

Rosa sighed. "We'll make a protective circle, then. Are you the only one home?"

Humphrey nodded. "Mom's at work. Dad is traveling this week. Bobbie's at her dance class for at least another hour."

"Good." Rosa tossed Jasper a length of string. He pressed one end to the marble floor while she used the other to draw a perfect and unbroken circle with a piece of chalk. Humphrey sputtered about marking up the floor. Rosa ignored him until the circle was done. Then she yanked him inside and snapped her fingers.

Light dimmed and grew fuzzy around them. The sound of rainfall faded.

"There," Rosa said. "You're safe. Nobody else can hear you."

The older boy did not seem calm, or comforted, to stand inside a sanctuary circle. His eyeballs looked like they wanted to leap out of their sockets and go hide all by themselves.

"Try not to bolt," Jasper said. "If you were a horse I'd put a blanket over your head and sing to you until you stopped freaking out. Would that work? Should I try it?"

Humphrey's face shifted from panicked to glowering. "You don't understand."

"Make us understand," Rosa said.

He tried. The words did not come easily. His voice seemed to crawl out of his mouth when he finally spoke. "My gran is haunting us. Grandmother Talcott."

"Your father's mom?" Rosa asked.

"No," he said. "My mom's mom. She kept her name, and passed it on to us. The mayors of Ingot have always been Talcotts."

"Good to know," Rosa said. "So what's wrong with a grandmotherly haunting? Most people have ancestors lingering around. Lullabies from *my* mom's mom are sewn right into the quilts she made."

"It isn't like that," Humphrey said. He made a face as though his own voice tasted bitter to him. "Gran was horrible. She's *still* horrible. Mom won't talk about her. She just says things like, 'We didn't have the easiest relationship,' and then changes the subject. She doesn't admit that her mother was horrible. But we know. We can tell. And now Gran is haunting Bobbie. She whispers in her ear. All the time. Insulting her. Cutting her down. Pinching her skin to make sure she gets her attention. Gran is probably at dance class right now, relentlessly criticizing every move that Bobbie makes. And the more she does it, the more . . . *alike* the two of them get." His face scrunched up as if he were struggling to hold on to his tears.

"I'm sorry," Rosa said, and she was, though she also

felt disappointed. *This doesn't sound like it has much to do with the voice-stealing water fountain.*

Humphrey turned on her, obviously mad about almost crying in front of witnesses. "It's your fault. You brought the hauntings back. Bobbie thinks we can make it all stop if we just get rid of you. Run you out of town on a rail."

Rosa felt a lot less sorry. "Do you know what that means? To run someone out of town on a rail? It was a kind of public torture. They'd strap you to a sharpened steel rail and then carry it bouncing through the streets to the edge of town, where they'd dump whatever bloody mess was left."

"Oh," Humphrey said. "Gross. It doesn't mean 'to put someone on a train and send them away'?"

"No," Rosa said. "It doesn't."

"How do you know that?"

"I've always lived in libraries. And I also know that sending me away would solve precisely none of your problems."

"Then tell me what would!" the older boy demanded. "But *don't* tell me that Gran needs to be appeased. Don't expect any of us to forgive her."

"Relax. I don't have any talent for forgiveness either." She rubbed the piece of chalk between her fingertips in a thoughtful sort of way. "Tell me more about your gran. Tell me what she loved."

"I don't care," Humphrey said.

"I'm not asking you to care," she told him. "I am asking you to tell me about things that your grandmother loved when she was alive."

"Hurting people," he said. "Making herself feel stronger by tearing her daughter and her granddaughter down."

"I believe you," Rosa said. "What else?"

"Nothing else."

"Come on. What else? Even cartoon supervillains love their pets, or their gold-plated furniture, or the portraits of themselves that they commission each year on their birthdays. I am already convinced that your grandmother was vile. Please also tell me about something that she loved."

Humphrey continued to glower. If *he* were a supervillain, Rosa felt certain he would drop her through a trapdoor and into a fighting pit filled with weredinosaur clones.

"I can help," she promised him. "But first you have to tell me what I need to know."

He looked away. His fingers cracked as he clenched them together. "The garden," he said. "Gran loved the garden."

"Excellent," Rosa said. She clapped her hands and

rubbed them fast as though trying to start a fire with a twig. "Did she have a favorite part of the garden? Or a favorite plant?"

"Tulips." Humphrey told her. "They're all gone. My dad tore them out."

"Perfect," said Rosa. "You need to plant some more. You'll also need a plaque or stone marker. It should have the usual sort of thing carved into it. 'In memory of Whatshername,' with birth and death dates. Something like that."

"We won't honor her," Humphrey insisted. "I won't forgive her."

Rosa tried to stay patient, but she made impatient noises. "I didn't say, 'In *loving* memory.' Pay attention. These words matter. This is all important. You need to set a marker in the ground next to some tulips. After that you need to say something, over and over and over again, right on that very spot. Your sister needs to say it, too."

She paused to make sure that he was listening.

"What?" he finally asked. "What do we need to say?"

"'This is yours, and nothing else.'"

"But I don't want to give her *anything*."

"I know," Rosa said. "You still have to. And you get to set the terms for exactly how you are willing to honor her. Give her this, and *only* this. She'll take it. She'll stop following Bobbie around and stay right there, inside that spot, if you dedicate it to her. 'This is yours, and nothing else.' *Nothing* else."

Humphrey sniffed. "That'll work?"

"Yes," she said. "It will. Do it soon. Plant those tulips. Nell MacMinnigan can probably forge a plaque for you."

"Okay," Humphrey said. "Thanks."

"Don't worry about it."

Rosa stepped outside the circle. The rainfall instantly became louder. She fetched a wet paper towel from the kitchen—which was a large, white, shiny place that looked clean enough to perform sterile surgeries on the countertop. That extreme level of cleanliness made Rosa feel like a germ. She hurried back and wiped away all evidence of chalk from the floor.

"Are you okay to stay here?" Jasper asked Humphrey. "You can come over to the farm instead."

"Or the library," Rosa suggested. "We can pretend to do homework."

"No," he said. "Thanks. But I should stay. I want to be here when Bobbie gets home."

"Okay," Rosa said. She dug a small vial of dark liquid out of her tool belt. "Here. Take this."

He didn't. "What is it?"

"Homemade ink mixed with saltwater. Use it to write notes to your sister. Tell her about the tulips. Your grandmother won't be able to read anything you write with this."

Humphrey took the vial as if he thought it might explode.

Rosa opened the front door and left.

"See you," Jasper said in a stoic sort of way, which felt like the right tone to use. It let them both ignore emotions that Humphrey clearly wanted to ignore.

"Bye," Humphrey said with equal stoicism. Then he shut the door.

🍂 14 🍂

JASPER AND ROSA STOOD ON THE FRONT PORCH OF
the Talcott family home. It was still raining.

"Well," she said, "that was a little bit satisfying. I
guess. But I don't see how their horrible grandmother
connects to any of the hauntings at school."

"Maybe they don't connect," he said. "The mayors
of Ingot have always been Talcotts. Always. So your
soggy notebook might have been talking about any gen-
eration of them, past or present."

Rosa sighed. "Time to hit the library, then. I'll
have to look at maps to see what's under the Lump,
and page through town records to find out about all
of those other Talcotts. Which means I'll have to talk

to Mrs. Jillynip. I don't *want* to talk to Mrs. Jillynip."

"We all have our burdens," Jasper said with mock sympathy.

Rosa made a *pbbbbbbbbbbt* noise at him. "Do you see those two royal ditch-diggers anywhere?"

"Geoff and Po," Jasper said. "And no, I don't. I think they're still hiding from the rain."

"Good. Let's go peek at the gardening cart that they were obviously trying to hide from us."

Punishing sheets of water continued to fall from the sky and pummel the ground.

"Rather not," Jasper said.

"Me neither," said Rosa.

"Ready, set, go," he said, and they went.

Rain almost knocked them over as they ran downhill. Sneakers slipped in the wet grass and mud. Momentum made it difficult to stop. They almost fell directly into the freshly dug ditch, but instead they skidded to a halt at the very edge.

Rosa looked down. "That looks pretty deep for an electric dog fence."

"How deep are dog fences supposed to be?" Jasper wondered.

"I have no idea," Rosa admitted. "But I'm suspicious anyway. Let's check the cart."

They crouched beside the gardening cart and lifted up a corner of the tarp.

Copper scrap was hidden beneath it. They saw pots, pans, pennies, and lengths of pipe all welded together. Some of the copper looked shiny and new. The rest was covered over with dark green patina.

The word "lethe" had been carefully etched into every piece.

"Barron's wall," Rosa whispered. "These are all salvaged bits of that circle. The Talcotts are making their own private banishment fence."

The sheer depths of her anger almost delighted her.

Rain calmed down to drips and drizzles. Car doors opened and shut nearby. The ditch-diggers were returning to work, so Jasper and Rosa bolted. They ran all the way back to the road and away.

It had stopped raining completely by the time they got to the library, but they were already soaked all the way down to the toes of their socks. They stood dripping in the front lobby while Rosa phoned her mom. "Hi. Are you home? Good. Can you bring a couple of big towels upstairs?"

Athena Díaz brought towels upstairs. She brought the bedraggled and towel-wrapped kids downstairs, put the kettle on, and went digging through boxes of old clothes for something dry that Jasper could wear.

Rosa squelched into her own room to get changed. The quilt on her bed hummed three or four different lullabies simultaneously. It sounded discordant. She still loved it.

"Thanks for not being horrible," she said to the echoes of her grandmother.

The quilt hummed happily in answer.

Rosa joined Mom and Jasper in the living room. Dozens of books loaned from other library branches filled up the place in unsettled piles. Mom had brought her work downstairs. Now she shifted those piles around to clear some couch space for Rosa and Jasper, and to clear the coffee table for steaming mugs of peppermint tea.

"Tell me your troubles," Mom said.

Rosa tried to tell her, but she couldn't, because she recognized the slacks and button-up shirt that Jasper had changed into. Both had once belonged to Rosa's father.

She gulped down a mouthful of tea so that she wouldn't have to say anything. Then she almost coughed it back up because the tea was still hot.

Jasper explained instead. "The Talcott house is badly haunted, so they're building a fence around it—a buried circle made out of copper."

"Ah," Mom said. "I'm not surprised. Nell and I found a patch of ground in the mountains where Barron's circle had been cleared away already. Now we know where all that missing copper went. The mayor is trying to make her own personal gated community between the living and the dead."

"You don't sound worried about that," Jasper noticed.

"Oh, I'm not," said Ms. Díaz. Then she went on to explain—a little *too* quickly—why she was not worried at all. "That fence isn't likely to work. Burying a bunch of metal that local ghosts are allergic to won't necessarily lock those ghosts out—not unless Mayor Talcott has trained for years in the forbidden arts of banishment. I'm pretty sure that she hasn't. But I'll go meet with her anyway, just to be safe. Maybe I can help her with home appeasements and talk her out of the whole thing."

"Rosa offered Humphrey some of that same help," Jasper said.

"Good."

Both of them glanced at Rosa. Rosa looked away and sipped her tea. It was still very hot.

"Good," Mom said again. "Jasper, are you staying for dinner? I've got some microwavable things that don't taste terrible. Or I could make pancakes. I might make pancakes. I did mean to get groceries today, but these irate piles of books have kept me busy."

"No thank you," Jasper said. He sensed Rosa's discontent, because he was Jasper. "Pancakes do sound good, but I should get home."

He leaned sideways to bump his shoulder against Rosa's, which meant *See you tomorrow*, and also, *We'll be able to handle whatever haunted nonsense tomorrow brings*.

She understood, and pushed back with her own shoulder. That meant *See you tomorrow*, and also, *I'm sorry that the unexpected sight of my father's old clothes are making it difficult for me to breathe*.

Jasper probably didn't catch the second part. He left with a plastic bag full of his own soaked clothing.

"What's wrong?" Mom asked once they were alone.

Rosa didn't answer right away. Instead she picked up a pile of unhappy books and tried to help sort them. Her mother did the same. They made separate stacks of the books that refused to open, the books that kept swapping sad and happy endings back and forth, and the books that pushed subtext too close to the surface.

Mom tried to soothe a novel badly haunted by early and unpublished versions of itself by reading the first page aloud. She savored the words as they were, and tried to quiet the haunting drafts of the words as they weren't.

Rosa started a new pile for outdated nonfiction. One

battered book with an orange cover was sulking because it insisted on disproven facts about dinosaurs. She tried to soothe its pride and wondered what it might be like to do appeasement work in a natural history museum. Then she set it down with another science book that still called Pluto a planet.

"Pass the glue," Mom asked. Rosa passed her the glue. Mom repaired a book that remembered being a tree. It sprouted leaf buds every spring and shed them every fall. That took a toll on the binding.

"Is Dad haunting you?" Rosa asked suddenly.

Mom paused. Droplets of glue fell to the carpet. She didn't notice. Rosa did notice, but didn't do anything about it.

"No," Mom said. "He isn't, though I thought that he would. I expected him to follow me here, even though we did leave a proper memorial for him back in the city. I was braced for his haunting after Barron's wall came down. But I haven't seen or heard any sign of your father. The memorial must have worked."

Rosa shook her head. "He might be haunting me."

Her mother's hand slipped. A very big glob of glue landed on the carpet. She noticed this time, and scrambled to clean it. "What do you mean?" she asked as she scrubbed. "Have you heard his voice at all? Has he said anything?"

"No," Rosa said. "Nothing like that. I just see glimpses of him in the corner of my eye, or in other people's faces. Mostly my history teacher. But it might not be a real haunting. I don't think it is. I ought to be able to spot an actual ghost by now, so I really don't think it's him. But I'm not *completely* sure. I'm not even sure whether or not I want him to be there."

Mom reached over and pulled Rosa onto her lap. It was awkward. Athena Díaz was not tall. The two of them were practically the same size.

"I think you just got some glue on my shirt," Rosa said.

"Shush," said her mother. "Let me pretend that you're still tiny and snuggleable. And please, please tell me if you ever, *ever* hear your father's voice."

"Okay," Rosa said.

"Please. We'll make him another . . . memorial. If we have to."

"Okay," she said again.

Rosa very much wanted to feel comforted. But she didn't, because Mom was afraid, and Rosa had never known her mother to be frightened of anything.

15

JASPER GOT HOME AND SEARCHED FOR HIS PARENTS. Neither one of them seemed to be anywhere nearby. He suspected that both were out in the stables, and almost went looking for them there. Instead he took up his quarterstaff, put on a pair of sturdy boots, and went squelching across the fairgrounds to the festival gates.

He felt completely incapable of standing still. Things were happening in his hometown—large, important, and unmanageable things. Jasper didn't know what he could do to affect any of them. But Handisher the tortoise was still missing, so at least he could go searching for Handisher.

Inside the gates it felt several degrees colder. Ice

clung to the edges of mud puddles. Frost covered the fallen leaves that new festival ghosts used to remake themselves.

Several leaf people crunched and crackled as they moved from stall to shuttered stall in the marketplace. If Jasper came too close they flinched away suddenly, alarmed by the copper coins on his staff, so he tried not to get too close.

"I didn't come to pick a fight." Nothing and no one responded to him. Maybe they had forgotten the use of their voices. Maybe they remembered and chose to ignore him. Maybe they never had any voices to begin with. Jasper felt as if he were the one haunting this place rather than the other way around—like he lingered here, and maybe he shouldn't.

Something made out of braided tree saplings went by, its roots moving together like centipede legs. Four young foxes sat in the upper branches. Jasper couldn't tell if those fox kits were a part of the haunted thing's new body, or if they were hitching a ride.

Dozens of ghosts in mining caps crouched together on the Tacky Tavern roof. There wasn't enough room for all of them, so they climbed up onto each other's shoulders to perch like awkward birds. Headlamp beams swept back and forth in slow unison like searchlights. Jasper kept clear of them.

He searched the muddy ground for tortoise tracks. This felt like a useless and futile thing to do. Handisher was obviously gone. Either the tortoise had wandered off into the woods to live a wild life, or else ghosts had taken him apart as building material to make new bodies for themselves. Whatever fate had befallen Handisher, he clearly wasn't here.

Jasper kept looking anyway. That tortoise was a festival mascot, last seen draped in royal livery. He was no one and everyone's pet. The urchins had looked after him together. As the child of festival directors, Jasper had always been first among urchins, so it was still his responsibility to find out what had happened to their tortoise.

Piles of loaned books continued to clench their covers together unhappily. Rosa needed to get away from them all. She also needed to put some distance between herself and the unfamiliar, unsettling awareness of her mother's fears.

She went upstairs and into the library proper. She didn't wear shoes, because her favorite pair was still wet. Mrs. Jillynip would probably berate her if she noticed Rosa shoeless in the library, so Rosa entertained herself by thinking up scathing responses that she might make if the older librarian disparaged her feet. But she didn't see Jillynip, so she didn't get to use any of them.

The coffeemaker in the back office started screaming. Rosa went behind the front desk to appease it. Then she went into Special Collections, signed the clipboard on the wall, and put on a pair of special white gloves.

"Maps, maps, maps," she said. Rolls of old paper crinkled beneath her gloved fingertips. "Talk to me. Show me what's buried under the Lump."

She hunched over drawings of Ingot and measured out tiny, imaginary miles to find the spot where the Lump was now. But the maps refused to tell her what it used to be. They showed only a small and unlabeled spot next to the schoolhouse.

Mrs. Jillynip came down the spiral staircase with a tea tray. Bartholomew Theosophras Barron had once haunted the apartments at the top of those stairs, but with the lord of the house now absent the local librarian had switched her care over to Lady Isabelle.

"Food and drink aren't allowed in Special Collections," Rosa said. She couldn't resist picking a fight.

Mrs. Jillynip raised one aggressive eyebrow but refused to take the bait. She glanced over Rosa's shoulder. "What are you doing, barefoot child?"

Rosa rolled up one map and then unrolled another one. "I am not tearing up these priceless artifacts of our history in my frustration, and I am definitely not eating the torn pieces afterward."

"Glad to hear it." Jillynip said. "Tell me more about this frustration. You should ask a librarian whenever you have trouble finding something."

"I *am* a librarian," Rosa growled.

"Then you should know this already." Jillynip was enjoying herself. Every day she depended on Rosa's knowledge of ghosts and hauntings, but now she got to savor her own expertise instead. "Tell me what you are researching, please."

Rosa did not want any help. She did need it, though. "I'm trying to figure out what's wrong with the school. One of the water fountains is lashing out. And there's a lump of a hill behind the playground with a tree on top. That spot is very unhappily haunted. I need to know more about it. But the maps aren't helping."

"I see," said the older librarian. "Have you considered talking to someone who lived through the earliest days of our town history? Someone likely to remember what once stood on that very spot?"

"Maybe," Rosa admitted. "Yes. But I'd rather not."

"Her ladyship does appear to be in a good mood this afternoon," Jillynip said as she left with the tea tray. "I believe that she would enjoy more conversation."

Rosa glared at the staircase. She did not want to

climb it. She felt like the stairs led up to a diving board, one that towered high above a cold swimming pool. But she put away the maps, put away the gloves, and went up anyway.

16

JASPER'S SEARCH FOR THE TORTOISE BROUGHT HIM to the joust, just like it always did.

He stood in the midst of a large crowd of scarecrows. All of them moved with more confidence now. Knights and their steeds remembered themselves more clearly and remade themselves more skillfully. If Jasper squinted at them, or watched sideways, they almost looked like the living.

Beams of bright light scanned back and forth across the lists. The miners were watching. They had climbed down from the tavern roof. Now they spread out and grew in numbers to surround the joust.

Jasper felt a slow unease creep from the back of his

neck to the tips of his fingers. *They've always ignored each other*, he thought. But the mining dead and the festival ghosts did not ignore each other now.

Sir Morien noticed the new spectators. He broke away from the jousting loop and raised his lance high. The gesture might have been a greeting, or a question, or a challenge. It might have been all three of those things put together.

The miners seemed to take it as a challenge. They came swaggering closer. Jasper squinted in the glare of their surrounding headlamps.

Scarecrow knights, horses, and spectators shifted their attention outward. It felt like a change in the direction of the wind.

This is going to get ugly. Jasper drew a circle in half-frozen mud with the tip of his staff. Once inside he set himself apart.

A fight between conflicting histories broke out, broke open, and broke everything.

Rosa climbed up and into the library's upstairs apartment. These rooms were strangely shaped. Ceilings followed the irregular geometry of the roof right above them. Elegant furniture sat crammed into odd corners at uncomfortable angles. Stacks of paper covered a small dining room table. Diagrams, sketches, and the angular handwriting of Bartholomew Theosophras Barron covered the paper.

Many of those pages had been meticulously torn into shreds.

The apartment was still much cleaner than it used to be. Mom and Rosa had spent weeks making the lady of the house feel welcome here. But through all of that dusting and tidying the mess of paper always remained on the table.

Rosa offered a small curtsey to the paper pile.

"Lady Isabelle," she said, "I've come to call on you, and to ask for the honor and privilege of your conversation." Rosa almost choked on the next thing that she needed to say. "You may borrow my voice, if you wish."

The ghost of Isabelle Barron no longer had any voice of her own. She would need to use Rosa's. Once Isabelle had Rosa's voice in her possession she might decide to keep it and never give it back.

Scraps of paper stirred on the tabletop. They spilled over the side, onto the floor, and then spun together in a spiral. The spiral stood as a flowing gown. The lady of the house took shape inside it. She considered her visitor through a face made out of paper.

Rosa held out her hand, even though most of her instincts said, *Nope nope nope nope nope nope nope, let's run away now please.*

Isabelle took the offered hand with her own pale and papery fingers.

"Good afternoon, little librarian," the ghost said to Rosa with Rosa's own voice. "What would you care to discuss?"

"Good afternoon," Rosa said, relieved to be able to say anything at all. "Thank you for taking the time to speak with me. I have questions about the history of our town."

"And is this *our* town now, newcomer?" the ghost asked with the voice that they shared. "Have you acclimated to this place? Are you well accepted here?"

So it's like that, is it? Rosa thought.

"Well enough," she said with an extra scoop of frosted politeness on top.

"I am so utterly glad to hear it," said Isabelle. She smiled without showing teeth, which was fine with Rosa. She did not enjoy the sight of those individually sculpted paper teeth. "Is your mother likewise well?"

"Very well, thank you," said Rosa. "She sends her fond greetings."

With her voice, Rosa silently added. *Which is hers. Not yours. You can't take it, or keep it, not ever again. And you can't keep mine, either. Please, please, please don't take away mine.* She tried not to tighten her grip too much on the lady's paper hand.

"You may answer her with greetings of my own," Isabelle said. "Now share your questions with me. I will answer them, provided that the answers are still held in my remembrance. Neither dead nor living memories are fixed and certain things."

"I understand," said Rosa. "Tell me, do you remember the part of town where the school is now? You can see it from here, through that window."

Isabelle did not bother to look through the window. "I remember. It was always a school, for as long as Ingot has existed and has had children living in it. I founded that school, and I spent a great deal of my time there. The original building was very much smaller than the current one, but it stood in the very same place."

"That's good to know," said Rosa. Maybe this conversation was a good idea after all. "Do you remember what was right behind the schoolhouse? There's a lump of a hill on that spot now, with a single tree growing at the top."

Isabelle pulled her hand away. Rosa felt her voice tear away with it. She tried to shout out protests, but she couldn't say anything now.

"Yes, child," Isabelle thundered with Rosa's own voice. "I do remember."

17

JASPER STOOD INSIDE A HASTILY DRAWN CIRCLE, deep inside a ghostly battle, right inside the center of the festival grounds. He watched, trapped and helpless, while dead miners and knightly scarecrows tried to destroy each other completely. This wasn't just a brawl, or the half-playful tussle of a playground fight. This had none of the posture and bravado of horses feeling scrappy and trying to become the boss by biting at each other's flanks. This was cold violence without rules. It aimed to obliterate.

At first the miners seemed to be winning. They broke scarecrows into pieces with pickaxes and heavily gloved fists. Then they broke those pieces.

Festival ghosts tore open the locked prop cabinets and fought back. Stage swords and jousting lances found wooden hands willing to swing them. The weapons were blunt, but still heavy. Several miners fell. Some of them exploded. Their lingering dust smelled like pulverized stone and spent fireworks.

None of the clashing figures spoke, or yelled, or taunted each other. None of them cried out in pain as they fell. None of them had any voices.

Jasper watched scarecrows remake themselves from their own wreckage. Miners coalesced from clouds of burnt powder. They kept coming back. They kept on fighting. And Jasper was still trapped in the middle of it all. He wondered how long his mud circle would last.

One voice rose above the horrible crunching and trampling noise of the battle to shout Jasper's name.

Sir Dad had joined the fray. He wasn't properly dressed for the occasion. He wore muddy jeans and a flannel shirt. But he had brought his new longsword with him. The copper-inlayed steel moved like Dad's own personal whirlwind. Dozens of feuding ghosts on both sides broke apart in his wake.

Neither the miners nor the festival ghosts seemed to know what to do with Sir Dad. They had been focused exclusively on each other. But once aware of him they came at him with dagger, spear, sword, and pickax. Dad disappeared from view, surrounded.

Jasper charged out of his circle. He tried to fight his way to his father. Miners burst in burning dust when he swung through them with his copper-tipped quarterstaff. Scarecrows broke apart in front of him. But then both sides pressed closer. Jasper switched to short, sharp jabs and quick parries. Several ghosts tried to grab at his staff. Green fire flared when they touched copper. The haunted figures flinched, but they did not retreat. Jasper had very little room to move, and no room at all to swing the staff. He couldn't see his father, or hear him. He tried to call out, but choked on the scorched powder of the miners. Headlamps blinded him. Wooden limbs of enraged scarecrows pummeled him.

The pummeling suddenly stopped, because Sir Dad was there.

He had found a battered shield and used it now to ward off a pickax. Then he cleared room around Jasper with his sword. Four ghostly heads separated from their makeshift shoulders.

Jasper shifted his grip on the quarterstaff and made two precise jabs. The open space around them grew wider. The claustrophobic press of ghosts fell back.

Sir Dad and Jasper, the living knight and his squire, fought together now as though they had choreographed and rehearsed the whole battle. They had fenced in the backyard almost every single morning since Jasper was three years old and able to hold a wooden stick. They both knew every move that the other would make.

Miners and scarecrows fell away from them.

Father and son pushed through and broke free, untouchable.

Jasper laughed with a blood-singing joy. Then he slipped in a large mud puddle, dropped his staff, and went right down beside the Mousetrap Stage.

Panic galloped through him. He expected both haunted armies to dogpile right on top of him. Jasper scrambled for his quarterstaff and braced for that pile. But it didn't happen. The battle between miners and scarecrows continued to rage nearby, on the jousting grounds, but that was where it stayed.

"Come on," said Sir Dad. "They aren't following. We still need to hurry on out of here."

"Wait just a second. . . ." Jasper saw something move beneath the stage platform. He pulled away in case it was the sort of something that might reach out and grab him. Then he leaned closer to see what it was.

Handisher looked back. The living tortoise hunched under the stage, half-submerged in mud and munching on earthworms.

"Found you." Jasper yanked him out, which wasn't easy. The tortoise was heavy.

"Here, you take the shield," Dad said. "I'll take the tortoise."

They swapped. Handisher tucked his legs and scrunched his neck deep into his shell.

"Now run," Dad said. He used his ordinary voice to say it. Jasper half-expected his father to speak with the exalted tone and accent of Sir Morien. But his father wasn't performing now. He just had a job to do. That job was to protect his son. And also a tortoise. With a sword.

They ran, and almost made it freely through the gates.

Sir Morien stood there and blocked their way out.

The scarecrow knight thumped the flat of his sword against his own shield three times, as though beating a drum.

Dad set the tortoise down. Handisher peeked out of his shell, didn't like what he saw, and scrunched his head back in again.

"That's you," Jasper tried to explain. "I think he's upset. We both knocked a lot of other scarecrows down."

"I know exactly who and what that is," said Sir Dad. "I'll need my shield back. Now stay clear. Try to keep that tortoise from wandering off again."

"But—"

"Stay clear I said."

Jasper nodded.

Sir Dad and Sir Morien met at the festival gates.

18

SIR MORIEN WAS MADE OUT OF WOOD, CLOTH, AND memory. That was what he was, and *all* that he was. He had knit himself together from the echoes of every performance, from every time that Jasper's father had played that character over the course of twenty-odd summers. The scarecrow was the distillation of Sir Dad's knightly skills. His stance and his posture were absolutely perfect—whereas Dad seemed winded and spent after the battle on the jousting field.

"He's out of practice," Jasper whispered to Handisher. "He might lose. Dad might actually lose a fight with his own shadow."

The two knights clashed. They soon broke their

shields and dropped the useless, splintered wreckage as they circled each other. Master strikes flowed quickly between them, almost too fast for Jasper to see. The knights were not performing with wide, sweeping movements meant to be noticed by an audience. Sir Dad and Sir Morien fought only for each other.

Swords met in a bind and remained locked together. The duel became a wrestling match, exchanging weight and pressure with a single inch of steel as the point of lasting contact.

Dad stepped back, gave ground, and loosened the bind. Sir Morien pressed his advantage.

Jasper rushed in closer, desperate to distract the scarecrow. Both knights ignored him. Sir Dad stepped aside and used Sir Morien's momentum to bring his own blade swinging back. He struck at his opponent's cloth-made face with a Zwerchhau. Morien countered with an identical strike.

They got stuck in a whirligig. Zwerchhaus spun over their heads like helicopter blades. Then Dad broke the loop by crouching down and pummeling the scarecrow with the pommel of his sword.

Sir Morien broke in a burst of green light.

Rosa tried to grab Isabelle's hand, missed, and stumbled instead.

She tried to speak. She couldn't speak. No sounds took shape in her throat. No words took shape in her head, either. She couldn't think straight. Even the silent voice of her own private thoughts was gone.

Isabelle stood tall over Rosa, a swirling whirlwind of paper scraps and incandescent rage.

"I remember the scaffold that they built there," she said. "I remember the hole in the world that they made. It was a well, the very first well dug in Ingot. Cold, clean water flowed from it at first. But then it was made foul by the mine and the refinery. I died of drinking from it. So did most of the children who attended that school. We haunted my husband for that. We haunted the engineer who dug holes in the world for him. We cried 'Poison!' in their ears until they banished us and burned away the history of how we died, until our voices wore down to nubs of silence. But I do still remember the taste of that water, how cold and clean and clear it was at first, how vile it was after. I remember the well behind the schoolhouse. I have not forgotten it. I will not forget it."

The ghost reached down, took both of Rosa's hands, and helped her stand up again.

"Good," Rosa said. She almost sobbed to hear her own voice settle back where it belonged. "We'll make sure that the rest Ingot remembers, too. But if you ever, *ever* take my voice again I will drag all of your old belongings outside, burn them in the parking lot, and settle your haunting self into a dirty, ugly smear of memorial ashes on cracked pavement. Do you understand me?"

Isabelle smiled, this time with paper teeth. "I do understand you."

"Good." Rosa said again. She kept on repeating that word in her head, just because she could do that now. *Good good good good good.* "Help me out in return. Someone else is taking voices. In the school. Through the water fountain. Poisoned kids, I'm guessing?"

"That seems likely to me," Isabelle said. "I am glad to hear it."

"I'm not," said Rosa. "The living need those voices back."

Lady Isabelle shook her head. It twisted a little too far each time, as though her paper neck could not remember precisely how necks were supposed to work. "Listen to them. They will be heard. They must be heard."

"Okay, sure. I'll hear them out. But they haven't told me anything so far. Just the name 'Talcott.' What does that mean to you?"

"Talcott." The ghost spat out the name. "That was my husband's engineer. Franz Talcott. He built the mine and the refinery. He dug the poisoned well. He served as the first mayor of Ingot, and sired the family line of all the mayors that followed after. Those who died of the water he tainted have not forgotten his name."

"Aha," Rosa said. "*Now* we're getting warm. Do you know where I might track down Franz Talcott's haunting self?"

The whirlwind that was Isabelle had ceased to pay attention to her. "We will not forgot," she said again before she lost all cohesive form. Scraps of paper collapsed into a pile on the floor.

Rosa sighed, swept them up, and put the paper scraps back on the table.

Father and son stumbled up their own driveway.

Jasper kicked the stone steps of the front porch to say hello to household spirits, and also to knock some of the mud from his boots.

Several more knocks answered him. The pumpkin lanterns had settled a whole host of small wanderers underneath the porch.

Sir Dad took Handisher down from his shoulder and set him on the ground. The tortoise found earthworms to chew on, and chewed. Dad sat down hard on the top step.

"Let me see the sword," Jasper asked.

His father handed it over. Jasper examined the blade, which was very badly notched after the fight. An hour or two with a whetstone would fix some of the damage, but not all. Nell would have to take a hammer and anvil to the rest.

"How did I win?" Dad asked.

"You won because of your unsurpassed excellence at fifteenth-century swordplay," Jasper said. "There's no one better. Not since the fifteenth century was still happening."

"Probably true," Sir Dad admitted. "But that rag doll was just as good. He remembered every technique perfectly. And he didn't seem to get tired. *I'm* exhausted. So how did I win?"

Jasper leaned back, grateful for the chance to geek out about swords with his father. They hadn't done this in a while. "Maybe he remembered *too* perfectly."

"Aha," said Sir Dad, his voice both tired and pleased. "Meaning what?"

"Hauntings can get stuck in loops," Jasper said, thinking out loud. "The same thing happens on the same spot, over and over again. After the bind you got him stuck in a loop. Then you chose when and how to break it. And you broke him when you did."

"With the pommel." Dad tapped the heavy,

copper-inlaid circle at the base of the hilt. "Not the sort of thing I've ever done in stage combat. Hurts too much, even in armor. Pommels are heavy. And it's such a close move that an audience wouldn't be able to see it clearly—not unless they were right up front. Theatrically unsatisfying."

Jasper understood. "So if you had never really done that before—not there, at the festival, as Sir Morien—then he wouldn't remember it, or guard against it."

"Exactly." Dad took the sword back and carefully sheathed it. Then he looked sadly out across the field. "Do you think he's gone?"

"Sir Morien?" Jasper asked.

Dad nodded. "I played that knight for longer than you've been alive. Made him out of everything good that I know about chivalry. It's not about holding doors open. It isn't the genteel con of acting polite while taking other people's things, because you've got a horse and a sword and they don't. Or at least it shouldn't be. Chivalry was supposed to be a way to carry yourself when you know that you're stronger, and you refuse to use that strength viciously. It's a good ethic. One that I wanted to teach you. Plus it's been fun to strut bravely and swing swords around every summer. It's been a lot of fun. But now it's over. I won. We fought, I won, and it's over."

Jasper felt suddenly cold, as though haunted by something new. "I don't think he's gone. Ghosts don't just go away. He'll pull himself together and come back."

"Why do *you* keep going back there?" Dad asked. "Please don't. It's much more dangerous now."

"I needed to find Handisher," Jasper explained defensively.

"Now you've found him," Dad pointed out. "The tortoise is safe. So don't go back."

"I also need to understand what's happening there. I need to figure out how to fix it."

Dad laughed, but his laugh sounded small. "Understanding is the easy part. Reenactments never mix with the ghosts of real history. You should see the ugliness that goes down at Civil War sites whenever somebody tries to put on an old uniform. This right here is *nothing* in comparison. You can't lie about history, not in a place like that. The ghosts rise up to voice their objections. And Ingot was a mining town back in the day, not a walled medieval city. Our own ghosts have come home. They're searching for *their* home with lamps strapped to their foreheads. But this place isn't familiar to them. Now it's a fake medieval village occupied by a borrowed, warped, deliberately misremembered, and flat-out imaginary version of the past. And they don't like being misremembered. Smaller festivals can get away with that sort of thing, sometimes, in mildly haunted places. But this fest was the best and the biggest. We can't get away with it anymore."

Jasper didn't want to argue about this. He wanted the whole conversation to end, cease, and disappear. He wanted it to have never happened in the first place. "We'll fix it. We'll find a way to fix it."

Dad waved his sword at the stable. "We need to keep this farm running. That's difficult enough. Let those two sets of ghosts duke the matter out between them while we keep clear."

The screen door squeaked in protest when he opened it. It squeaked again as it shut.

Jasper stayed on the porch with the tortoise. He could still hear the clash and clamor of battle ringing out across the field.

NOVEMBER

19

ROSA KICKED THE FRONT STEPS OF JASPER'S PORCH
in the extremely early hours of the morning. She got
one answering knock. It sounded surprised. The living
weren't usually up so early, even on a farm. Sir Dad
no longer greeted the dawn with shows of swordsmanship.

Jasper came out to meet her. He carried his quarterstaff and one small pebble, which he tossed. Then
he made a quick tisking noise with the tip of his
tongue.

Stones gathered together on the spot where that one
pebble fell. Some tore up from the ground. Others skit-
tered over the gravel driveway.

Jerónimo reassembled himself and stamped one hoof.

"Hey there, Ronnie." Jasper reached out to stroke the pebbles of his haunted horse's face.

"Should I do that, too?" Rosa asked. "Try to pat his . . . snout? Nose? Whatever horses call it. Just to say hi."

"Probably not," Jasper advised. "Don't reach for his face until you know that he likes you."

"How will I know that?"

"You won't. At first. But you will definitely be able to tell if he *dislikes* you."

"Oh. Good."

Jasper used the porch steps to mount up onto Ronnie's back. He made sure the copper tips of his staff didn't touch the horse. Rosa took three tries to climb up behind him, but she finally did it.

"Ready?" he asked.

"No," she said. "Why can't we use a saddle?"

"Because Ronnie won't tolerate saddles anymore."

"Why can't we ride a different horse, then?"

"Because none of the living horses are willing to go where we're going."

"We could walk. Can't we walk? Maybe we should just walk."

"We'll be late for school if we walk all the way up there and back."

"Maybe that's okay," Rosa said. "We could be late. We should just be late."

"This was your idea," Jasper reminded her.

"I know," she said. "We've tried everything else, so we need to do this. But I still don't wanna."

Jasper didn't want to get where they were going either, but at least he felt fine with their method of travel. "Squeeze your knees together, but try not to tap Ronnie's sides with your heels. He'll go faster if you do that. Like this." He tapped and tisked again.

Ronnie took off trotting down to the end of the driveway. Rosa did not enjoy this. A trot was a bouncy and stuttering way to move.

After some weight shifts and heel taps the horse turned toward the mountains and took up a smoother, speedier, cantering gait.

Forest and fog thickened around them. Isabelle Road contracted to a mere dirt track. Leafless tree branches reached at the riders and brushed loud against the sleeves of their coats.

Ronnie slowed as the way grew steep. Dawn light crept uncomfortably through the fog and teased out the shapes of looming things moving between trees. Some of the looming, moving things *were* trees.

A bear with a boulder for a head watched eyelessly as they went by. It raised a paw in greeting.

Something made out of seven coyotes fell apart, ran separately across the track, and then stacked itself back together on the other side.

The riders reached a clearing, and a long gash in the ground.

Barron had built his copper circle here. He had banished all the rest of Ingot's dead to the other side of this line. But only Barron haunted the spot now. His scorched bones rested near the mouth of his old copper mine, underneath a pile of heavy stones that Nell and Rosa's mother had stacked over him. Then they had set a memorial plaque at the base of the stones. It read:

BARTHOLOMEW THEOSOPHRAS BARRON:
FOUNDER, ENTREPRENEUR, AND LETHEAN.
BE WELCOME HERE.
FIND WELCOME NOWHERE ELSE.

"What's a Lethean?" Jasper asked.

"Someone just as devoted to forgetting as librarians are to remembering," Rosa told him.

Jasper dismounted from the pile of stones that had stacked itself into his horse. Rosa tumbled down after him. Then the two specialists got to work. They lit candles, surrounded themselves with protective geometry, and called upon the town founder to come and chat.

Barron's bones climbed out from under the cairn, settled into place, and then took up handfuls of dust to shape into the semblance of flesh. Dead leaves crushed together became the strands of his long mustache.

"Lady Díaz." His voice was dry and gentlemanly. "Young Master Chevalier."

Rosa stepped up to the edge of their circle. She very much wanted her sword, but Barron might not have agreed to speak with them if she'd brought the blade that had once cut off his hand. And she really didn't know what to expect of this conversation, or what sort of grudge the town founder might hold against them for the next thousand years. Rosa and Jasper had personally shattered the work of his life, and the work of his death, when they brought all other hauntings home to Ingot.

"Good morning, sir," she said. "Thank you for speaking with us. It's very gracious of you." Barron enjoyed respectful flattery.

"I do not often receive visitors," he said. "Except lately. How is our fair town in the valley below?"

"Well enough," said Rosa.

"Is it?" Barron snorted, which scattered his mustache. He made himself another. "Is it as comfortable a place as it appears from this far distance? Are all the citizens content? Or do I hear the grumblings of division?"

"We're getting used to the new state of things," Jasper said.

Barron ignored him. He spoke only to Rosa. "How does my own dear wife enjoy her accommodations?"

"Better than her old ones," Rosa said with a knife-twisting smile. "Lady Isabelle sends her fond greetings."

"Yes, I am certain that she does." Barron stretched. His bones rediscovered their habits of fitting together. "Now then, to what do I owe the very great pleasure of your visit? Is it merely to deliver regards from my wife? If so, you may bring my own back with you. I hope that she enjoys watching the town we built tear itself apart. Ingot has begun to remember things best left forgotten."

Rosa parried and struck back. "I will tell her that you said so. I do suspect, however, that she finds more satisfaction in remembrance than amnesia."

Barron destroyed his mustache with another snort. He gathered leaves and made a third one. Then he drew shapes in the dirt with one bony fingertip.

Rosa switched back to flattery. "Sir, we've come to ask for details from your own memory. As the founder of Ingot, you know more about this place than anyone, dead or living."

"I cannot deny that," the dead man agreed. "What

does your youthful curiosity desire to learn?"

She started to tell him, but then Jasper cut in.

"Tell us about the open field to the west of town." He pointed, though none of them could see the fairgrounds through the trees and fog. "What was it like before, when Ingot was new?"

The dead man rustled his leafy mustache.

"Please tell us," Rosa said, though she wasn't sure why Jasper had asked.

"Music," said Barron without looking up. "I remember the music. They held dances there, in the old meeting hall, once in midsummer and once in midwinter. I understand that those were the two most terrible times for refinery work, the former being too hot and the latter too cold, so in that time they danced to relieve their difficulties. Franz played piano, as I recall."

"Franz Talcott?" Rosa asked. "The engineer?"

"Yes. The very man. Quite capable. He became our first mayor. They offered the position to me, of course, but I declined." He drew more marks in the dirt. "You should know that you are not the first to come with questions about Franz, and about the projects that we accomplished together—including the great barrier that once stood on this very spot. I consider this a very curious coincidence."

Rosa considered it curious, too. "Who else was

here? Mayor Talcott? I mean the *living* mayor, not any of the other ones." Rosa's mother had already tried to gently discourage the mayor from building a copper fence around the Talcott family home, but that hadn't worked—which was probably fine, since the fence itself wasn't likely to work, either.

Unless they ask questions of those who practiced and perfected the forbidden arts of banishment in Ingot, Rosa realized. *If they do that, then they might figure out how to make the fence work. And that would be bad.*

"No," the dead man said. "It was not she. Nor any other she. I did not recognize him. And he spoke to me imperiously, which I did not care for, so I answered very few of his pestering questions."

Rosa was relieved. She tried to keep from sounding imperious herself. "Did your other visitor also ask about the well? The *first* well, dug near the schoolhouse?"

Barron looked up sharply.

"I remember the taste of that water," he said. "Clean and clear. Shockingly cold. So cold it hurt the teeth to drink. And *very* clean. We chose the spot carefully. He assured me that no runoff from the mine would ever reach it. No waste from the refinery would touch that water. It was clean. Clear. And so very cold." He scraped hard in the dirt with his fingers, agitated now.

"Then it was poisoned," Rosa said, tiptoeing closer to things that she needed to know.

"It was *not* poisoned." Barron's dry voice twisted with inhuman sounds. Ronnie reared up, kicked the air, and shied sideways away. "Franz assured me that this was so. Good water flowed from the well he made, smooth as music, clean and pure. He promised me this. But they would not listen, the dear ones who fell ill. And she would not listen. No peace until I silenced them. No peace until forgetting." He tore a length of iron rail from the ground, a relic of the old mining carts, and used both hands to twist it into the shape of a jagged blade.

Rosa held one hand high and snapped her fingers.

Look up here! the gesture said.

Barron looked up at her hand.

"Now," said Jasper.

Rosa jumped. Jasper swung low with the quarterstaff. It passed under Rosa's feet and knocked the dead man's legs out from under him.

He fell apart as he hit the ground.

"Thank you for your time," Rosa said politely to the pile of bones.

The specialists gathered up those bones and stacked the cairn over them again.

"Was that useful?" Jasper asked. He soothed the

agitated Ronnie with another sugar cube.

"Maybe," Rosa said. "I'm not sure yet. We need to figure out who else is asking about banishment. It has to be somebody connected to the Talcotts, right? They're the ones still trying to do it." She extinguished all the candles, stuffed them in her coat pocket, and immediately regretted it when hot wax spilled on her hand. "Ow."

Jasper used a fallen tree as a step and mounted up. Rosa scrambled after him.

"What was that about the fairgrounds?" she asked him.

He shrugged. "Just something my dad said about the ghosts of old Ingot. They're searching for the place they remember, and not finding it, because we made up a bunch of medieval memories to play around with instead. I'm trying to sort out what that bit of land was like when they were still alive, before it was a fake village. Maybe we can give them something familiar, something that welcomes them home. Maybe we can find a way to give them what they want."

"Maybe . . . ," Rosa said. "But they seem to want the festival gone. Completely and utterly. Two different sets of memories are trying to coexist. And they don't like each other very much."

"They really don't," he admitted. He clicked his

tongue twice to ask Ronnie to move. The haunted horse stepped carefully away from Barron's cairn.

Jasper's stomach growled.

"I skipped breakfast, too," Rosa said. "Do we have time to eat something before school starts?"

"If we hurry."

"Never mind. Hurrying seems dangerous."

"Says the specialist who just stood unarmed before her enemy."

Rosa didn't respond. She had already closed her eyes and clenched her teeth together.

Jasper clicked his tongue again and nudged with his heels.

The stones that were Jerónimo cantered quickly down the mountainside.

❧ 20 ❧

RONNIE SCATTERED HIMSELF NEXT TO THE LIBRARY parking lot. Jasper pocketed one of the fallen pebbles while Rosa unlocked the back door.

The two specialists snuck into the apartment down-stairs. Jasper stashed his quarterstaff in a corner of the living room behind some moving boxes full of books that hadn't been unpacked yet.

Mom stuck her head through the kitchen doorway. "You two were up early."

"Research trip," Rosa said.

"Learn anything useful?"

"Maybe."

"If we knew what we were doing, then it wouldn't be

called research," Mom pointed out. "Need breakfast?"

"Yes," Jasper said. "Very much. Please. Yes."

Mom filled up their extra-large toaster with bagels and heated up some café con leche that was mostly leche. Then she turned on the kitchen radio. Static hissed, crackled, and murmured words in dead languages like Latin and Sanskrit. Mom turned the dial and found the weather report, which announced that it would soon begin to snizzle outside. None of them had ever heard the word "snizzle" before. They argued about what it might mean.

"Sounds like boiling rain sizzling when it hits pavement," Rosa said.

"Boiling rain would be a good reason to stay home from school," Jasper said.

The toaster dinged. The specialists stuffed their faces full of warm, buttered bagel.

"Hey Mom," Rosa started to say.

"Don't talk with your mouth full," Mom said with her mouth full.

"Barron told us that someone came asking questions about banishment and how it works. Someone living. He didn't recognize them, so they weren't anybody local."

Mom choked on her bagel. She had to spit some of it back onto her plate. "He said *what*? And you spoke to Barron without me? Don't ever do that."

"It was fine!" Rosa insisted. "We're fine. I mean, he did try to kill us with a rusty iron rail. But we handled it."

Mom invoked her middle name. "Rosa. Ramona. Díaz."

"I'm sorry," Rosa said quickly. "We won't go chat with Barron again. Not alone. Not without you."

"Promise," Mom insisted.

"I promise," Rosa said.

"Good." Mom took a long drink of her caffeinated milk.

Her hands shook. Jasper noticed. "Do you know who else went to talk to him, Ms. Díaz?" he asked gently.

"No," she said. "Not if it was someone living, and from out of town. The Talcotts wouldn't know how to summon Barron, and they would be too terrified to try. But I do know exactly what sort of person would want to have that kind of conversation."

"Who?" Rosa asked. "Who could possibly be that stupid?"

Mom folded her hands "Dearest daughter, you tend to think that everyone knows and agrees with the basic tenets of appeasement—in this case, that banishment is bad and doesn't really work."

"Right," Rosa said. "I do. It's obvious."

"Not to everybody."

"They're wrong," Rosa said. "Every time. Look at Ingot."

"People *do* look at Ingot. They scrutinize and study Ingot. A successful banishment circle stood here for more than a hundred years."

"And then it failed," Rosa said.

"And then you ended it," Mom said. "The two of you ended it. Bravely. Wonderfully. But who knows how long it might have lasted otherwise?"

Rosa felt the molten core of herself spin faster. "About five minutes, I'm guessing."

"Less," Jasper said.

"*You* know that," her mother said, "and I know that you're both right. But some would disagree." She finished her café, poured another, and kept her voice carefully even. "When librarians work alone we end up wandering through deserts with a donkey-drawn cart full of outlawed books. When we work together and get organized we build magnificent libraries like the ones in Alexandria and Tenochtitlán. But either way, we keep the world's memory." Mom sat back down. "Banishment is usually practiced alone, by someone desperate to make a single haunting go away." Rosa looked at the floor and tried not to think about her father. "But sometimes forgetters get organized, band together, build walls, and burn the libraries of Alexandria and Tenochtitlán."

"Letheans," Jasper and Rosa both said at once.

"Letheans," said Athena Díaz. "We light candles to read by. They light books on fire. And they are very interested in Barron's circle—interested enough to summon up his ghost to ask him how he made it."

The radio lost its signal and slipped back into staticky Sanskrit. Mom turned it off.

"You're both going to be late for school," she said. "Off you go. I need to call up some friends at the Library of Congress, tell them that Lethean things are still actively happening in Ingot. Then I need to see the mayor. If her little copper fence is a desperate act of amateur banishment, we have nothing to worry about. But she might be getting more knowledgeable help."

"How can we possibly go to school with all of that happening?" Rosa demanded.

Mom shook her head. "If you skip school today you'll just bounce around our apartment, eager to pick a fight. That would be good for neither of us. Go to school. Tend to those classroom hauntings. That's where you're needed."

"But—"

"Rosa. That is where you need to be. That is what I need you to do."

Jasper and Rosa walked to school in the snizzle, which turned out to be a relentlessly drizzling mixture of snow and semifrozen rain.

They reached the schoolyard and checked to see what the King of the Lump was up to. It still hid inside a whirlwind. Fallen leaves had not fallen any farther. Snizzle clumped those leaves together as they spun.

Rosa threw a slushball at the Lump. It joined the spinning leaves and spun right along with them.

"You can't keep hiding in there forever," she said. "Speak up already. Why would you steal a whole swack of voices if you're not going to use them to say anything?"

Nothing responded to her words or her slushball.

School buses disgorged students at the front entrance. Rosa and Jasper kept to the very back of the crowd, and the crowd moved to keep well clear of them. No one wanted to be knocked over by the inhospitable door.

Cold snizzle assaulted their faces while they waited.

"Have you gone back to the festival grounds?" Rosa asked.

"No," Jasper said. "Not for weeks. But I know

they're still fighting. I can hear them at night, and see the glow of all those headlamps."

"They might start to use ice and snow for bodies now that they have some to work with. Dozens and dozens of snowmen locked in an endless fight that neither side can win. Or maybe they're snizzlemen now." She tried not to laugh. A grim sort of giggle escaped from her anyway.

"You're ridiculous." Jasper didn't want to laugh either, but it was contagious.

"Beware the never-ending battle of the snizzlemen!" Rosa picked up a stick and waved it in the air.

The other students hurried indoors and away from the snizzle until only Rosa and Jasper were left.

"Let me see that?" he asked. She handed him the stick.

The front door tried to slam shut as they approached. Jasper threw the stick. It got stuck, pinned between the door and its threshold. Rosa used it as a pry bar to lever the entrance back open. They went through. The door closed in a sulking sort of way.

21

MORNING CLASSES PASSED SLOWLY AND WITHOUT any serious hauntings. This was frustrating. Rosa itched for a problem that she knew how to fix.

She checked in on the history classroom right before lunch. It was dusty and unused. All of Mr. Lucius's classes were held in the school library now. A poster of James Baldwin smiled down at her and insisted that *History is longer, larger, more various, more beautiful, and more terrible than anything anyone has ever said about it.*

Rosa put down a coin on the tray below the chalkboard, picked up a red piece of chalk, and tried to start a conversation. *Hello. My name is Rosa. Please talk to me.*

She waited until the lunch bell rang. Nothing on the other side of the chalkboard answered her.

"Rage," she said softly to herself, just to gain a little power over the sudden surge of feeling by naming it. "Frustration. Disgruntlement."

We never use the word gruntlement, she thought. *Does anyone ever feel gruntled? That should be the opposite of disgruntled, but it doesn't sound like a good feeling.*

She set out a fresh bowl of rabbit food for Lafayette and left.

The lunch line was already long by the time Rosa got to the cafeteria. She took her place at the end, right behind the Talcott siblings. Both of them forcefully ignored her. Neither had spoken to Rosa, or even made eye contact, since she had offered Humphrey appeasement advice. That was fine by her. She was usually content to keep her distance. But today Rosa had crawled out of bed very early on a cold and snizzly morning. She had confronted Bartholomew Theosophras Barron unarmed. And she had learned that Letheans were likely here in Ingot, trying to perfect their ways of poking holes in the world's memory. Rosa was in no mood to be ignored.

"Humphrey," she said.

He pretended not to hear her, but he wasn't very good at pretending.

"Humphrey Hieronymus Talcott." Rosa had been itching to say his middle name aloud ever since she'd found out what it was.

Both siblings turned halfway to look back at her. Bobbie wore a thick scarf around her neck even though the cafeteria felt uncomfortably warm.

"Do any gardening lately?" Rosa asked.

"What are you talking about?" It wasn't really a question. Humphrey turned back around before she could answer him.

Guess not. Rosa thought. *Oh well. Not my problem. Unless you learn how to finish your cowardly copper fence, and I will become* your *problem if that ever happens.*

Bobbie did not look away. She maintained a steady glare as though still trying to win a staring contest. Rosa offered an answering glare. But then she noticed movement in the fabric of Bobbie's scarf. It clumped around her neck in handlike shapes. Rosa saw bruises peeking out from beneath those fabric hands.

"Turn away," said a harsh, dry whisper. "Don't look at her. Don't associate with her."

Bobbie turned away. She coughed as the scarf continued to tighten around her throat. But she stood tall and made sure that no one else noticed her suffer—not if they didn't already know what to look for, and how to look for it.

Ick, Rosa thought. *You're still carrying around a vicious grandmother. Okay. Maybe I can find a way to make this my problem.*

Jasper was already seated at the quiet table along with Gladys-Marie and all six silenced students. They still couldn't speak. They also couldn't write. A voice can express itself in writing, and voice was something that they no longer had. Mike couldn't sign anymore, either. Both of his parents were deaf, so his hands had always been fluent, but now both hands were as empty of words as his voice box.

The six couldn't do schoolwork, but they still came to school and stuck together.

Rosa joined them.

Jasper nodded *hello*, but said nothing aloud. No one spoke at the quiet table—not even those who still could.

He took a bite from his sandwich. It turned out to be a good and lucky thing that he had chosen a sandwich instead of the soup.

Gladys-Marie got up and waved Rosa over to the wall, well away from the table-size cone of silence. Rosa was hungry, but she left her food tray next to Jasper and followed Gladys-Marie to a place where they could talk.

"I'm sorry it's taking me so long to get your sister's

voice back," she whispered. "I think I know who took them all. But so far they haven't used those voices to say anything, which is frustrating and weird. But I'm trying. I'm sorry."

Gladys-Marie crossed her arms like they made some kind of armor. "Don't be sorry," she said. "Just tell me if there's something I can do. Choir auditions are next week, and Tracey really wants to sing. Can the two of us *share* a voice? Or swap? Is there some kind of voice transplant that we can work out?"

"Maybe . . . ," Rosa said, considering the idea. "It's trickier to do between two *living* people. But maybe. I'll look into it."

"Thanks," Gladys-Marie said. She started to say something else, but never got to it.

The cafeteria chatter grew strangely quiet, and then very loud. Trays clattered as other students stood up quickly, mouths open. They tried to shout. Nothing happened, so they just tried harder. Others pointed at them and shouted instead.

Rosa stared at her panicking schoolmates as they struggled to speak, or shout, or scream. She remembered what it had felt like when Isabelle had torn her own words away. For one long and thin-stretched moment she relived that memory as if it were still happening, and would always be happening.

Then it ended. She made it end by pulling the fire alarm.

Everyone knew what to do next. Flailing uncertainty fell away as the cafeteria full of students lined up in silence, marched outside, and waited there without coats. A snizzling misery settled over them.

Teachers counted students and gathered up strays—except for the teachers who had eaten the soup and couldn't speak, or count, or read their attendance lists.

Jasper tried to explain things to the firefighters who had shown up expecting some sort of fire to fight. The chief seemed extremely uncomfortable with the nature of the actual emergency. "Ghosts got into the kitchen water and haunted the soup?" Luckily the chief was also captain of the royal guard in summertime, so Jasper knew him and how best to talk to him.

Rosa's heart beat to a faster tempo than she would have liked, but her earlier shock had faded. Mostly. She noticed that Englebert the Awful had sipped some of the soup himself, and she savored a moment of delight at his misfortune.

Mrs. Smoot, the assistant principal, called Rosa's name. Mr. Ahmed was with her. He still came to work every day, even though he couldn't do any principaling until he got his own voice back.

"Hi," Rosa said.

"Hello, Miss Díaz," said Mrs. Smoot. "Do you have any clear notion about what happened here?"

"Yes. I think a bunch of child-ghosts from an old well got into the kitchen water and took voices away from everyone who ate the soup. But I don't know what they want with all of those voices. They aren't very talkative."

"I see." Mrs. Smoot had a high and sugar-coated voice. Rosa sometimes wondered if she might be a ghost who remade herself out of marshmallows. "If the water itself is so badly tainted, then we will have to close the school until the matter is resolved."

Rosa nodded vigorously. "I think so, too."

"And how long do you think it will take to resolve this, exactly?"

Rosa pointed at the Lump. "Until I get through that mulchy whirlwind over there and flush out whatever is hiding inside it."

"How do you plan to do that?" asked Mrs. Smoot.

"I really don't know," said Rosa, but she said it with courage and determination.

The assistant principal sighed. "We'll discuss this later, then. Right now I need to mobilize school buses, get everyone home, and explain haunted water to several dozen unhappy parents." She went away to do her principaling. Mr. Ahmed went silently with her.

Rosa watched the Lump and the wet leaves that still spun around it. "Just. Tell. Me. What. You. Want," she growled. "How many more voices do you all need to confiscate before you remember how to use a single one of them?"

A loud car engine growled and popped nearby. Nell's truck drove up to the sidewalk in a sudden spray of slush puddle. She rolled her window partway down—which was as far down as it ever went—and shouted at Rosa through the three-inch gap. "Get in! We've got an emergency."

"I've got an emergency already unfolding right here!" Rosa told her.

"Is your school on fire?" Nell asked.

"No," Rosa said.

"Is anyone trapped inside it?"

"No one living."

"Then your emergency is less of an immediate emergency than my emergency," Nell said. "It's the *Talcott* place, understand? Your mother is there already."

Oh crap. Rosa yanked the door open and jumped into the truck.

Bobbie and Humphrey overheard and came running.

"What was that about my house?" Bobbie demanded.

"Climb in," Nell said. "All of you. And you too, Chevalier!"

Jasper left the discombobulated fire chief to join them. All four kids squished uncomfortably together.

"We don't have enough seat belts," Bobbie complained. "We can't buckle in. And the whole fire department is standing right there watching us. You'll get some sort of reckless endangerment ticket."

"I'm not worried." Nell said as she shifted gears. "Chief still owes me money from poker night."

Bobbie was not mollified. "Gambling debts won't save us if you crash into something."

"Guess not," Nell said. "I'll try not to crash." She punched the gas hard and lurched away from the curb.

22

ROSA SAT NEXT TO BOBBIE. THIS PLEASED NEITHER of them.

"What happened?" Rosa asked Nell, which helped her ignore everyone else.

"They got the fence working," Nell said.

"Good," said Bobbie.

"Bad," said Rosa. "Very, very bad. You should have just planted those stupid tulips."

"I *did* plant tulips," Humphrey admitted. "Just like you said. But I couldn't get Bobbie to go through with the rest of it."

"We don't *need* to go through with the rest of it." Bobbie said smugly. "We don't need to make any sort of memorial. The fence is done. Finally. Our house won't be haunted anymore."

"You're wrong," Rosa said. "If that banishment fence really is done, then pretty soon your house won't be *standing* anymore."

Finger-shaped folds in the scarf tightened. Bobbie coughed. Rosa heard the softly vicious sound of her grandmother's whispers.

She snuck a pinch of salt from her tool belt and casually flicked it behind Bobbie's head. The whispering sputtered and stopped.

Nell pulled up at the bottom of the Talcotts' long driveway. She couldn't get any closer. A long trench cut across the driveway asphalt. The mayor and her husband stood on the far side of that trench. Geoff and Po were with them. Both landscapers carried their shovels like spears.

Athena Díaz stood outside that circle. Many ghosts joined her there. Household revenants, echoes of ancestors, spirits of mirror reflections, and the ghosts that lurked in every latch, window, and threshold had been cast out of the house at the top of the hill. Now they made bodies for themselves from the mud and gravel unearthed by ditch-digging. They made mouths and eyes to hold wide open in their misery.

"What is your mother doing?" Bobbie demanded.

"Is she trying to break our fence?"

"No," Rosa said. Her voice sounded calm. That surprised her. "Mom is holding your fence together. She knows what will happen as soon as it breaks."

She climbed right over Bobbie, Humphrey, and Jasper to get out of the truck. Then she wove carefully between the ghostly figures to stand at her mother's side.

Mom had her eyes closed and her hands open. She recited the Litany of the Seventh Lyceum over and over and over again. Her forehead was sweaty, even though it was cold. Snizzle still fell from the sky.

I'm here, Rosa didn't speak out loud. She didn't want to distract her mom. *I'm here to help.*

Other people became very loud and distracting. The mayor called out for her children to join them inside the circle, where she thought it would be safe. Bobbie and Humphrey tried to jump over the ditch. They failed, because Bobbie fell down screaming. Humphrey couldn't help her get back on her feet.

"Let me go!" she cried out. She wasn't talking to her brother. Her scarf writhed around her throat.

"You are *mine*," whispered a harsh, husky voice behind her. "You are mine. And you have locked me out of my own house, you miserable, ungrateful, undeserving thing."

Mom started up the litany again. Her hands shook.

Do something, Rosa told herself. She tried to stay calm in the midst of the chaos and noise.

"Better do something," Nell said. "Or else tell me what to do. Tell me how to help your mother. Anything. Quick."

Rosa's own pumping blood was magma in her veins. She couldn't tell how much of her rage properly belonged to her, and how much of it was borrowed from the displaced ghosts around her.

"Should we cross over?" Jasper asked. "I could try to hold the circle together from the other side."

"No," Rosa told him. "Please no. You could, but don't. This bubble of a barrier is going to pop at any moment and you'll die if you're inside when that happens."

Barron had spent most of his life and all of his death perfecting the banishment circle that once surrounded Ingot. This slipshod fence was far less perfect. It wouldn't hold. It couldn't hold. The circle would break. Every banished ghost would come rushing home again, and the force of that homecoming would leave nothing standing inside.

Rosa had seen it happen before.

"Can we break this circle *carefully*?" Jasper asked. "Just like last time?"

"We can't," Rosa said. "*We* can't. Because we don't live there." Then she understood what needed to happen. "But Humphrey and Bobbie could do it. The wall might not come crashing down if they invite their ghosts to cross over and come home." She raised her voice. "Did you hear that? Bobbie? Humphrey? If you want to keep your house and parents then you should help us break this fence."

Humphrey looked helpless and bewildered.

Bobbie glared her absolute refusal. She tried to say something, but the tightening scarf wouldn't let her say much.

Bursts of coppery green fire flared up from the trench. "Too late anyway," Rosa said. "Nell, can you just yank them out?"

The mayor and her husband held their hands out to Bobbie and Humphrey, still imploring both of them to come inside. Nell reached over the barrier, grabbed those hands, and pulled them out. Mr. and Mrs. Talcott sprawled in the mud, surrounded by the muddy figures of their ancestors.

"Geoff and Po!" Nell called out. "Move!"

The landscapers looked terrified, but they dropped their shovels and jumped across the trench that they had made.

Rosa heard her mother's voice catch and stumble.

The circle broke.

Time stretched itself thin. Wind and fire tumbled inward as the banished ghosts came home. Every tree, blade of grass, and carefully trimmed garden shrubbery became scattered ashes in their wake.

Rosa looked up. She saw the house on the hill in its very last moment, right before it collapsed.

She saw her father standing on the porch.

Then he was gone, and so was the porch, and so was the house.

❧ 23 ❧

TEN PEOPLE STOOD OUTSIDE THE BROKEN COPPER
fence.

Nothing and no one stood inside it.

The Talcott family home had been reduced to an
unrecognizable pile of rubble. Household spirits pieced
themselves together from the pieces that they found
there.

Rosa stared at the wreckage, afraid to blink or
breathe.

*What did I just see? It was him. I saw him. He was
there. Haunting the threshold of the house, right before
everything else that should have been properly haunting
that house knocked it down. I saw him. But was it really*

him? Was that just a jumbled memory of the last time I watched this happen, when his own foolish bit of banishment collapsed around his library, and so did the library, all of the books and brick walls crumbling down around him? I was outside. Across the street. On a swing. Doing nothing but sitting there. Mom made it out, all scraped and bloody, but he didn't. That's how he died. This is how he died. Maybe I only saw him just now because I wanted to, because I needed to give him another chance to get out before the circle broke. But it's too late. His circle already broke. He's already gone.

Her mother stood up, dusted her hands, and sighed.

Geoff and Po mumbled some hasty condolences. Then they ran away.

The living Talcotts huddled together and gaped at the place where they used to live.

Rosa tried to tell Bobbie that she was sorry. She tried not to say *I told you so*. But Bobbie cut her off before she could say either.

"This is your fault," the other girl said. Her eyes hardened like two pale puddles freezing over. "All of it is your fault."

Rosa turned right around and got back into Nell's truck.

She wanted to sharpen her own words into icepicks and use them to explain, with brutal precision, that

Bobbie's parents had been rescued from the death that Rosa's father got. But Rosa didn't say anything. Instead she waited for her mother, Nell, and Jasper to join her. Then she spent the whole drive home carefully crafting, polishing, and sharpening the points of everything she wished she had said.

Once there Nell built a fire in the library's big stone fireplace. Smoke wraiths danced over the logs as they caught and blazed. Jasper and Rosa sat on the floor, right next to the hearthstone, until the snizzle-induced chill began to leave their feet and fingers.

Some wraiths made bodies for themselves out of fire.

"That one moves like Tim," Rosa said, pointing.

"Who's Tim?" Jasper asked.

"A dance choreographer. He used to volunteer at our old library, back in the city. I don't think it *is* Tim. I'm pretty sure he's still alive. And he knows exactly which theater he means to haunt after he dies, so he wouldn't come here. But that little fire ghost does move like him. Sort of."

Her voice sounded as flat as a sheet of blank paper.

Mrs. Jillynip bustled over to make sure that they didn't accidentally burn down the whole building.

"The weather report now calls for thundersnow," she said. "Honestly. It said that 'snizzle will gradually become thundersnow this afternoon.' I truly do not know what that means." She went fretting away again.

"That sounds like a terrible name for a band," Jasper said. He strummed an imaginary guitar. *"Thundersnow."*

Rosa laughed a very little bit.

"Have I made you listen to Zwerchhau Whirligig yet?"

"No," Rosa said. "I have never listened to . . . Zwerk Ow Whirligig."

"Zwerchhau. They're pretty good."

"Okay."

Behind them, away from the fire and near the magazine rack, Rosa's mother tried to have a grown-up conversation with Nell. They didn't try very hard. The kids could still hear them.

"Will the mayor blame us for what just happened?" Nell asked. "Will she blame you?"

"No," Athena said. "I mean yes. Probably. But it won't matter. There's too much evidence of what really happened. And I've already called for backup from banishment experts and research librarians. They'll get here tomorrow. Maybe even later today, if we're lucky. Then we'll track down whoever helped them put that misguided fence together."

"Good," Nell said. "What do you need in the meantime? Anything?"

"Nothing," said Athena. "No, wait. That's not true. Takeout? Burgers? We might need burgers. I can't bear to microwave dinner tonight."

"Burgers," Nell said. "Check. I'll be back with burgers." She tapped the top of Jasper's head on her way to the lobby. "Come with me, Chevalier. Let me drive you home through all of that wintery mix. You need to check in with your parents before they hear about the day's chaos and worry that you got caught up in it. Which you did. So I should get you home."

She gave Jasper a Significant Look to also suggest that the Díaz ladies needed to be alone.

He understood. "I'll see you later."

"Okay," Rosa said.

Her voice still sounded thin. Jasper wanted to know why, but she had closed and shuttered all the doors and windows of her face. "Send word when you need backup."

"Okay," she said again.

Nell and Jasper left.

Athena Díaz knelt on the floor next to her daughter. They pressed their shoulders together and watched more wraiths make bright new bodies for themselves.

"That one move like Tim," Rosa said. "See?"

"I do see," said Mom. "But I don't think it's him."

"Me neither," Rosa said.

"Tim plans to benevolently haunt a whole theater when he dies."

"I know," Rosa said. "It isn't really him. It just looks like him. Sort of. And that keeps happening to me. With Dad. I saw him again today. Maybe. But I don't know whether or not that was really him, either."

Her mother's whole body stiffened. "Where?"

"Back at the mayor's house."

Mom nodded, very slowly. "That might have really been your father."

Rosa felt strangely relieved to have that confirmed. "But why?" she asked. "Is it because he died the same way? Doing the same thing? Bumbling into some clumsy banishment to get rid of a ghost that he just couldn't handle?"

"That's not how your father died."

Those few words caught Rosa completely off balance and shifted the shape of the world.

"What did you say?"

"That's not how he died." Mom said again. She closed her eyes. Then she opened them quickly as though she didn't like what she saw behind her eyelids. "He didn't foolishly dabble in just a little bit of forbidden banishment. He was devoted to it."

"How do you know that?" Rosa's whisper was almost too small to hear, but Mom heard anyway.

"I found books he kept hidden. Most were about Ingot. *The Unhaunted Valley*. *The Transcribed Notebooks of B.T. Barron*. *A Natural History of Banishment* has two whole chapters about this little town, and those chapters were full of margin notes and Post-its. He was a dedicated Lethean. And he was obsessed with Ingot. He wanted to learn how to do what Barron did here."

Rosa did not want to hear this. She didn't want to know any more about it. *Stop it*, she thought. *Stop talking. Please stop talking now.*

"What happened?" she asked aloud.

"You were outside," Mom said. "Sitting on a swing in the playground across the street. I saw you through the window. Then he saw me paging through his copy of *Unhaunted Valley*, reading his notes and understanding what they meant. I confronted him. We fought."

"Argued?" Rosa asked.

"No. Dueled. With swords and with circles. All up and down that library. He wasn't bungling or clumsy like we always thought—and always made excuses for. Your father was good at his craft. But it was the wrong craft. And he almost won. Almost. I had all the memories of that place on my side. All of the books were with me. But he had forgetting. He tried to get the whole world to forget me. If that had worked, then you wouldn't have remembered your mother at all.

You would have seen both of your parents walk into that library, watched your father walk out later, and believed forever afterward that I had died in childbirth or something. He tried to *erase* me. Instead he brought the building down around us both. You saw me get out before the whole place fell. He didn't. That is how he died. We fought. We dueled. I won."

Logs broke apart in the fireplace with a crackling, spark-scattering noise. Wraiths danced among the sparks.

"Of course you won," Rosa said. "You're the best specialist alive."

Mom kissed the top of her head. "Thank you, my heart."

Rosa considered the new shape that the world had shifted into. "So that's why we moved to Ingot?"

"Yes," Mom said.

"I thought we were just hiding here."

"We were also hiding here," Mom admitted. "We moved for good, important reasons: to learn more about a place so beloved of Letheans, and to protect that place before Barron's circle collapsed—because of course it was going to do that *eventually*. I didn't know that it would break almost as soon as we got here, though. I thought we would have more time. And that's the selfish reason why we came here. To hide."

"From Dad."

"Yes. From the ghost of your father. I wasn't prepared to confront him again. Not yet. Good doctors are usually bad patients. Good specialists still have trouble with their own hauntings. I'm sorry. I just wasn't ready."

"Don't be sorry," Rosa said. "You should have told me, though."

"No," Mom said. "I shouldn't have. Not then. You had a kind and clumsy father to mourn. It wasn't the right time to tell you about the man he really was. You weren't ready to hear it. But I think you are now. I hope so. Because he seems to be haunting you instead of me."

Rosa cracked her knuckles. "He is welcome to try."

24

THUNDER RUMBLED UP IN THE MOUNTAINS. Lightning flashed and crackled between the snow-filled clouds. The windshield wipers of Nell's pickup squeaked as they shoveled wet, heavy flakes aside.

"How are your parents?" Nell asked.

"Fine," Jasper said.

"Really?"

"No," he said. "Neither one of them thinks we can save the festival."

"Really," Nell said. "Huh. That's no good. Your parents are usually made out of optimism."

"Not this time," Jasper said.

"And what do *you* think?"

He stared out the window and tried to decide how to answer. "I don't know. Two sets of ghosts are fighting over the fairgrounds, and maybe they always will until one version of history completely annihilates the other one. And we can't have a festival while that's happening around us. We can't sell lemonade, swords, and roasted turkey legs to tourists while ghost miners attack us for erasing them with our made-up history. Both versions can't haunt the same place at the same time."

Nell pulled into the driveway of the Chevalier family farm. She parked and idled there. The windshield wipers struggled back and forth.

Jasper unbuckled his seatbelt, but otherwise he didn't move. Something itched at the back of his brain.

Both sides want to haunt the same place at the same time, he thought. *The same place. It has to be the same place. But does it have to be at the same time?*

"I need to find a way to get their attention," he said out loud.

"Your parents?" Nell asked.

"No. Not my parents. The ghosts at the fairgrounds. All of them at once."

She tapped a steady drumbeat on the steering wheel with her fingers. "That should be easy enough for the festival crowd. I imagine that trumpets and a royal fanfare would do the trick. But I don't know what might capture the other side's attention."

"They move their helmet lamps like searchlights . . . ," Jasper said, thinking out loud. "Dad thinks they're just looking for home. The way the field used to be. Trying to find something familiar."

"Go look for some old stuff, then. The refinery, the town meeting hall, and everything else at that end of Ingot got torn down years and years ago. But I bet you can find fragments for sale in Mildred Grün's antique shop. If they recognize it, then they might pay a little bit of attention to you."

Jasper buckled his seatbelt again. "Can I have another ride?"

A silver bell rang inside Grün's Antiques as Jasper went in.

Mildred stood behind the counter, sorting a display case of dangly earrings. She was tiny, white, and absolutely ancient. But there didn't seem to be anything brittle about her. If she ever fell down the front stairs Jasper figured that the impact would probably break the stairs rather than any part of Mildred. If she died in her sleep then she would likely wake right up on the following morning, open her shop at the proper time, and gradually build a new body for herself out of various antique oddments.

Maybe that had happened already. Jasper peered closely at Mildred.

"Are you checking to make sure that I'm still alive, child?" she asked without looking up from the earring display.

"No, Mrs. Grün," he lied quickly.

"Good. If you're here about some ghostly business, then you might have words with the pair currently inhabiting my ceiling. They are throwing a set of bone-handled knives between them."

"What makes you think I'm here on ghostly business?" Jasper asked. Her sharp assumptions made him want to be cagey.

"You run with the specialists now, I hear. Soaked up some of their knowledge. Is that right?"

"Could be," he said. "I might know those two poltergeists, too. They never drop anything."

"It still makes me a mite uncomfortable to see knives flying over my head," said Mildred. "If you could settle them down, I would be very much obliged."

Jasper took five flyers for the Renaissance Festival from a stack next to the cash register. Each one showed a full-color picture of Sir Dad in midjoust. He had the visor of his helmet down, but Jasper still knew him by his armor, the crest of his shield, and the posture of confident joy.

He crumpled up the flyers. Then he tossed the five paper balls in the air, one by one, and juggled while he picked his way carefully to the back of the store. Antique things paused their habitual whispers as he went by.

The two poltergeists did *not* pause, but they did include Jasper in their game by throwing knives at him. He caught those knives and tossed crumpled paper back. Then he bowed out of the game to bring the full set of knives back to Mildred.

She took them gratefully. "Now, what can I help you with? You have the look of someone searching for a very specific thing."

"Maybe," Jasper said. "I need to find something old and local."

"Well, take your pick. That describes almost everything here."

He shook his head. "Something from the old refinery. Or the meeting hall. Something from way back when Ingot was founded."

Mildred thoughtfully tapped on the side of her face. "Not too many want to remember that there was a copper refinery here, even now that all those ghosts are coming home. But I never did have trouble with that kind of amnesia. Quite enough copper in this shop to nudge a body's memory." She reached out one thin finger and pointed. "You might try looking on that shelf.

That one there. Behind the card catalogue, but before you get to the comics."

Jasper searched through the things on that shelf. He found a tin bucket full of lost keys without locks, a racist board game about cowboys, and a set of porcelain dolls that didn't seem to be haunted but unsettled him more than any haunted thing ever had.

He also found a bell the size of a volleyball. It dangled from a short length of chain, empty and clapperless, but it was made out of copper. The metal had covered itself with a dark green patina. Jasper could still read Barron's name stamped on the side.

I think this is it. He brought it back to Mildred and set it on the counter.

She considered the bell and flipped over its little paper price tag, which read $300 in precise handwriting. Jasper felt hope sink back down to ground level.

"This was from the refinery, sure enough. They rang it to mark break times, and the very end of the workday. But I'm guessing that you don't have the funds for it."

"I don't," he admitted. "I'll have to offer a swap."

Mildred folded her age-speckled hands. "I'm listening."

Jasper tried to think quickly. "I could bring over a crate of used horseshoes."

"Those do sell," she said. "Especially to tourists looking for small souvenirs. Not so many tourists come to town now, though. Not with the festival closed and unlikely to reopen. Besides, your folks usually *donate* their crates full of horseshoes to my shop."

Jasper clenched his teeth over the words "unlikely to reopen," but he didn't argue. "I can offer a mint condition copy of *Ultimate Fallout* Number Four."

"Interesting." Mildred typed a quick search into her phone. "Very interesting. And valuable. Plus I haven't read that comic yet. But it still isn't enough. Not quite."

"I also helped with your poltergeist problem," Jasper pointed out.

"True," Mildred said. "Answer me one question, then. Share more of that ghostly knowledge you've accumulated and we'll call it a swap."

Jasper tented his fingertips together. "I'm listening."

"Good. There's a child comes in here lately. A ghostly one. Little girl trying to track down her favorite doll. She finds it, too. I keep it out for her, and I don't let anyone else buy it. But she always leaves the doll behind when she goes, and comes looking again the next day. That isn't the strangest thing, though. What I can't quite sort out is the fact that I remember this girl. Gertrude was her name. We grew up together, and *she did grow up*. Lived to a respectable eighty-nine years of age. But now, when she comes haunting, she haunts as a child instead of someone well and truly grown. Why? Can you unravel that for me?"

Jasper thought hard about it. "Could be an injury," he mused. "Some kinds of hurt keep you locked in a place that you never really leave."

"Interesting" Mildred said. "Is that what you think is going on here?"

"No," said Jasper. "I think maybe there's a time when you come into your own. When you're most fully yourself. Sometimes you hold on to that through every other age, even when the rest of you changes."

Mildred looked pleased. "Now *that* could be. That could well be. Gertrude was always delightfully child-ish, as I recall. And this makes me wonder about the age of my own true self. I'm probably supposed to say that I am really seventeen at heart, and always have been. But truthfully, I don't think that I've reached my proper age. Not yet. Feels like I am getting close, though." She took a small pair of scissors and snipped the bell's price tag away. "I like your answer. Bring me the comic and you have yourself a swap."

"Thank you, Mrs. Grün."

"No thanks needed. And no need to rush. I do promise to hold on to that comic and keep it off the rack for a good long while, just in case you'd like to swap something back for it. What exactly do you mean to use that bell for in the meantime?"

Jasper tapped the bell with his thumbnail and listened to its distant-sounding ring. "What it was always used for."

25

ROSA'S MOTHER WENT DOWNSTAIRS TO TAKE A shower, because contact with banishment always felt icky to her. But first she planned to make more phone calls and coordinate the coming reinforcements of specialist librarians.

The grown-ups were mobilizing. The problems would be solved. Mom had promised. She insisted that Rosa didn't need to worry about rogue Letheans—living or dead, strangers or family. Nope. Not at all. Definitely not.

Rosa stayed upstairs by the fire. She knew that she should feel hungry. The cafeteria evacuation had interrupted her lunch. The breakfast bagel felt like a ghostly echo from centuries ago. But Rosa did not feel hungry.

Her stomach had forgotten what food was for. Maybe it would remember when Nell returned with grease-stained paper bags from the Tiny Diner, but right now Rosa had no appetite at all.

The fire settled down to become a bed of glowing coals. One wraith still danced above it.

Rosa scooted closer. She felt waves of heat against her face.

"Hi Tim," she said. "I don't know what your real name was. I don't know if you remember it, either. But I'd like to keep calling you Tim if that's okay with you."

The fiery ghost flickered and bowed.

"I could see you more clearly if I had a worry stone. That's a flat rock with a hole in the middle. I've got one in my backpack. But my backpack is back at the school. Which is closed and locked. Because the ghosts inside snatched dozens of voices today. And they won't talk to me. I'm responsible for that place. Mom is dealing with the library, and the town, and all sorts of Lethean things. All I need to do is handle the school hauntings. That's it. But I can't. Why won't those poisoned kids talk to me? What the absolute and unmitigated crap is the point of taking so many voices if you're just going to sit on them and stay quiet? It doesn't make any *sense*."

Mrs. Jillynip made a shushing noise from behind the front desk.

Rosa lowered her voice. "It doesn't make sense," she said again.

Her own words took one step sideways inside her head. *It really doesn't. No sense at all. Which means that something else is going on.*

She pulled out her phone as though drawing a sword. Texting thumbs moved fast over the screen.

We need to get back to the school, she told Jasper. Now. Right now. Right this very now.

Ok, he answered. It'll be locked, tho. And that building never likes to let you in.

I'll convince it, Rosa typed. Meet me there?

Meet you there.

She put her phone away. Tim continued to hover above the glowing fireplace coals, his posture and movements attentive.

Rosa reached out a hand. "Come with me? I need help from someone small and nimble."

The wraith jumped from the fireplace to hover above her palm. She cupped both hands to shelter him. It felt uncomfortably warm, but not quite burning.

"Thank you," she said.

Rosa left the library and walked to school through a snowy thunderstorm while carrying a ghost made out of fire.

She had work to do. This gave her something to

think about, something important—something other than her father's embarrassed smile. Had he always faked that smile? He didn't just dabble in banishments. He hadn't fumbled his way into dying.

Rosa walked faster to outrun that smile.

Jasper stood shivering at the front entrance of the school. He held a large paper bag, and he didn't have a coat. Neither did Rosa. Both of their coats were still locked inside.

"What's in the bag?" she asked.

"A copper bell," he said. "What's in your hand?"

"Tim," she said.

"Hello Tim," said Jasper.

Rosa held the ghost up to the doorknob. Reflections of his firelight danced against the metal.

"This threshold has an unreasonable dislike for me," she told him. "I can respect a grudge, but I can't have this. I'm the specialist here. Doorways and boundaries are therefore my territory. Please explain this to the door and lock."

Tim disappeared into the keyhole. Then he blazed back out. Rosa caught him with one hand.

The door unlatched itself and slowly opened.

"Excellent," said Jasper. "Shouldn't we have come armed, though?"

"Probably," Rosa said. "But I was in a hurry."

Every time she paused to think, the only thing she could think about was her father's embarrassed and bumbling shrug of a smile.

"We could go back for sword and staff," Jasper suggested.

Rosa shook her head. "Something wanted to empty out the school today. Something other than hauntings in need of a voice. Why? What? It might be too late to find out already."

They grabbed their backpacks from homeroom on their way to the haunted water fountain, which still wore Jasper's OUT OF ORDER sign. Rosa searched her pack for a pocketknife. Then she remembered her promise to Principal Ahmed and deeply regretted keeping it.

"Do you have a screwdriver?" she asked. "Or Duncan's phone number? We need to open this up and search its innards."

"Nope," Jasper said. "Neither. Do access panels on water fountains count as thresholds and therefore a part of your proper territory?"

"Don't make fun of me, Chevalier. And no. Not really. That's mostly doors, windows, and mirrors. Things we use all the time."

"Could Tim fit in there and pop it open?"

"Aha!" Rosa said. "Probably." She held the wraith

up to the fountain. "Would you mind? Be careful in there. Don't get yourself extinguished."

Tim slipped inside and rattled at the screws. It took time. The metal panel was hot to the touch by the time they pried it open. The wraith triumphantly lit up the space inside.

Tiny words and symbols had been etched into all of the plumbing.

"Does that word look like 'lethe' to you?" Rosa asked.

"That word looks like 'lethe' to me," Jasper said.

"But why would Letheans want to attack a school?" she said, thinking out loud. "I do get why they would study banishment circles, how they work, and the things that happen when they stop working. It's all horribly misguided and wrong, but I still get why they'd try. But why would they attack a school?"

Footsteps squeaked against the wooden floor behind them.

The specialists looked up.

Bobbie and Humphrey Talcott looked down.

"I knew it," Bobbie said, hands on hips as if she were a schoolteacher.

Rosa and Jasper both stood up slowly.

"Can we help you?" Rosa asked, though she made the words sound like a formal challenge. *Do not stand so close to us. Do not even share our air without permission. Step aside or be prepared to bleed.*

"You're the one who poisoned the water," Bobbie said. "You silenced all those other students."

"Nope," said Rosa.

"You destroyed our house!" The word "house" echoed in the yawning hallway.

"Untrue," said Rosa. "We did save both of your parents, though. You're welcome."

"And now you're breaking into the school."

"So are you," Rosa pointed out. "And what are you doing here, exactly?"

"Following you," Bobbie said. Her voice was a trumpet on the battlefield, triumphant and loud. "Proving that all of this is your fault. Are you poisoning the water again, or else trying to burn the building down?"

"Neither," said Rosa. "Your flamethrower-wielding brother is the pyromaniac here. Not us."

"Then *why is your hand on fire?*" Bobbie demanded.

"This is Tim," Rosa said calmly. "Say hello, Tim." The fire that was Tim bowed to the Talcott siblings.

Bobbie looked like she wanted to tie Rosa to a stake, make a pile of forbidden books at her feet, and then set fire to her like a martyred librarian in days of old.

"And now goodbye," Rosa said. "I really don't have time for you." She hoisted her backpack over one shoulder and brought Tim inside the history classroom to search for more signs of Lethean sabotage.

The other kids followed her. Bobbie continued to sputter, obviously brimming with righteous anger. Rosa knew how good that felt. But she also knew what it felt like to borrow the feeling from somebody else.

"You're still carrying your grandmother around," she said while looking for hidden inscriptions underneath the chalkboard eraser tray. "She didn't knock your house down with the rest of the household spirits, did she? Gran wasn't ever haunting that house. Just you. And she's still got you. She's whispering at you right now, isn't she?"

Bobbie opened her mouth to start yelling. Then she stopped, and pointed.

A lone piece of chalk hovered in front of the board. It scratched out the letters of a name with slow, deliberate, squeak-making marks.

Talcott.

"The two of you really shouldn't have followed us in here," Jasper whispered.

"What's going on?" Humphrey asked. His voice sounded brittle and skittish.

"Your ancestor poisoned a lot of kids," Rosa told him, her voice cold as she dropped facts at his feet. "After that Franz Talcott helped Barron engineer a way to banish all the ghosts who haunted them both. So those poisoned kids might hold a grudge against anyone with your family name."

"I don't understand anything that you just said," Bobbie complained.

Rosa shrugged. "Your ignorance is not my problem."

The air around them dropped down to a temperature colder than Rosa's voice.

"It's quickly becoming our problem," Jasper said. He grabbed two chalkboard erasers and whacked them together. Chalk dust billowed throughout the room.

It settled down into the shapes of children.

Some chalky figures sat at their desks. Others climbed on top of their desks. More stood on the floor, the walls, and the ceiling. A boy knelt on the chalkboard as though sideways were down. He held the hovering chalk that had written the name Talcott.

"Our ancestor killed them?" Humphrey whispered.

"He did," Rosa said. "We should probably run."

They ran.

26

THE FOUR KIDS FLED TO THE CAFETERIA.

Folding lunch tables were still there, still unfolded, and still covered with lunch trays of abandoned, half-eaten food. The room smelled like stale yuck.

Rosa, Jasper, Bobbie, and Humphrey dodged between tables on their way to the exit doors.

"Stop!" Rosa shouted.

They came to a tumbling stop in the center of the room.

"What is it?" Bobbie demanded.

"They're blocking the exit," Rosa said. "Look. Floating chalk dust. See?"

"No," said Bobbie. "It's dark in here and I can't see any floating chalk dust."

Rosa dropped her backpack. It made a loud and punctuating thunk against the floor. "Jasper, would you please hold Tim for me?"

The wraith leaped from Rosa to Jasper, who held his hand high and scanned the cafeteria by Tim-light.

Humphrey flinched away. Jasper smiled. He enjoyed carrying a handful of flame near the kid who had once tried to burn him.

Rosa rooted around in her backpack, dumped half of it on the floor, and finally found a small, flat rock with a hole in it. She gave it to Humphrey. "Here. This is a worry stone. Use it to take a peek around us."

"It's a what?" Bobbie demanded to know.

"A. Worry. Stone. You worry away the middle to make the hole. Then you look through that hole to see if there's anything nearby you need to worry about. Start looking."

Humphrey looked.

"We're surrounded," he whispered. "Kids. Dead kids. Our age. They're all around the room. Holding hands. Making a big circle all around us. We can't get out. They're all dead and we can't get out."

"Breathe," Rosa suggested. "Are they closing in on us? Getting closer?"

"No," Humphrey said. "They're just standing there. Facing away from us."

"Wait, what?" Rosa said, surprised. "They're doing what? Are you sure?"

"I'm sure. They've all got their backs turned."

"What does that mean?" Bobbie demanded.

"Probably nothing," Rosa said. "Never mind. Humphrey, just keep looking. Tell me if they do anything different."

Humphrey kept looking.

He flinched when he looked at his sister.

Notice that? Jasper asked with eye contact.

Rosa nodded.

They got to work. She took one particular piece of string and handed it to Jasper. He used a thumbtack to pin it to the wooden floor and held it there, perfectly still.

"What are you doing?" Bobbie asked. She tugged at her scarf with one finger, but the cloth only tightened in response.

"Is that a specific question, or a general one?" Rosa tightened the other end of the string around a particular piece of chalk. "Or are you just venting because you don't understand what's happening, and you don't like being told what to do?"

"All of the above," Bobbie said.

"Thought so," said Rosa. "What I'm doing is drawing a circle identical to one I made before, in my room. Same chalk. Same string. Same size. I need what's hiding inside that other circle, so I need to convince them both that they're really the same. Which is difficult. But I was in a rush when I came here, and didn't come fully prepared, and that was very, very stupid of me. Does anyone know which way is north?"

No one answered her.

"You're all local!" Rosa said, exasperated. "Bobbie, you're so very *proud* of being local! If this is your town, and you know it so well, then how can you *not* know where north is? I need a compass. Where is my compass . . . ?" She searched around in the mess of specialist supplies, but couldn't find it. Then she tried to picture all of those old library maps in her head, took a guess, and marked north, south, east, and west. Rosa reached for the eastern side where the hilt should be.

Please work, please work, please work.

It didn't. Her hand held empty air. She erased the four compass points and made new ones. The circle remained empty.

Bobbie knelt to help search for the compass, and found it. "That way!" she said. "North is that way."

Rosa made four new marks on the circumference of the circle. She closed her eyes and reached inside. This time her fingers closed around the hilt.

The weight of her sword felt perfect as she lifted it up. Tim's reflected firelight danced across the blade.

Humphrey gulped. "The ghosts are coming closer. They still have their backs turned to us, but they're tightening the circle."

"Step inside the one I just made," she told him. "It's small. There's only room for the two of you. But it might keep you safe."

Humphrey hesitated. "Are you sure? We made a circle around our house. That went badly."

"Because you tried to make it permanent," Rosa explained, exasperated.

He stepped inside. Bobbie tried to follow him, but she couldn't cross the line of chalk. She tried again. Humphrey didn't notice. He poured all of his attention through the stone ring and the surrounding ghosts.

"Are you going to fight them all?" he asked.

"Nope," Rosa said. "Hopefully they'll notice that Jasper and I aren't named Talcott."

"Hopefully," Jasper agreed. He shifted Tim to his left hand and took the bell from its shopping bag with his right. Local ghosts did not enjoy the touch of copper, so if it came to a fight then at least he could swing the bell around.

"We came here to talk to them," Rosa went on.

"Someone has been stopping me from talking to them. We need to figure out who that is." She took up a fighting stance. Her blade cut the air with a sound like a breath. "But it helps if they know that I'm dangerous."

"Everyone knows that you're dangerous," Bobbie said. She sounded frustrated and scared. She still couldn't step inside the small, chalk-drawn sanctuary.

"Thank you," said Rosa.

"You're welcome."

"I also needed my sword to do this."

Rosa took a swing at Bobbie's head.

27

BOBBIE SCREAMED IN ANGER AND SURPRISE.

So did her grandmother.

Rosa struck between the two of them, close enough to shave the fine hairs on the back of Bobbie's neck. She pivoted, pushed, and pried away the scarf with the blade of her sword.

"Get in the circle," Rosa told her. "Now you can."

Bobbie stumbled inside and almost knocked her brother out. They squished uncomfortably close together in the very small space.

"I can't hear her," Bobbie whispered. She touched the bruises on her neck as she stared at the inert puddle of scarf on the ground. "I couldn't tell the difference between her voice and my own thoughts anymore. But now I can't hear her."

"You're welcome," said Rosa.

"You could have warned me," Bobbie said.

"Not without warning *her*. And then it wouldn't have worked."

The scarf twitched. It twisted and writhed until the middle knotted itself into the rough shape of a head, neck, and shoulders. The two ends of the scarf became long, reaching arms. It lacked the fabric to make any more of a body, so the half-figure floated up to hover at Rosa's eye level. Wisp light glowed in the folded hollows of its eye sockets.

"You tore down my ancestral home," Gran hissed at Rosa with distilled hatred. "You will never belong here. Get out of Ingot. Go back where you came from."

Rosa and Jasper stood closer together. Tim put up tiny and fiery fists in Jasper's left hand.

"Sorry I can't summon up another weapon," Rosa said.

Jasper swung the bell like a mace from its length of chain. "I'll manage."

The specialists separated. They tried to flank the hostile ghost, to surround her and trap her between the bell and the sword. But Gran moved too quickly. She

sculpted the fabric of her hands into sharp, hardened claws and lashed out at them.

"She's over there!" the Talcott siblings shouted. "Right over there!"

"We *know* where she is!" Rosa shouted back. "Shush and let us focus!"

Craft your time, Catalina de Erauso wrote centuries ago. *Time is made by motion. Make your own. Do not allow your opponent to take it from you.*

Rosa tried to be patient. She tried to take her time, and to take it away from the vengeful scarf. But Gran easily avoided every strike. Her claws bloodied Jasper's arm and raked a gash across Rosa's forehead.

"We tore out your tulips," Bobbie said.

Gran stopped, hovered, and listened.

"Dad did most of the work," Bobbie went on. "He took them out carefully, one by one, and planted roses there instead. After that we took down the cheesy, hideous painting you kept in the living room. Humphrey and I drew all over it. We made dinosaurs stomp across that landscape. Then we sold it for five dollars at our neighbors' garage sale. You hated our neighbors. We used the money to buy the kind of ice cream that you never let us get. And ever since then Mom hasn't said a single thing about you. Not one unkind word, or any other kind of word. We forgot you. We were happy to forget you. When you came back we tried to build a fence around the house to keep you out."

The scarf-made figure turned to face her grandchildren. "You cannot cut me out of you. You cannot drain the blood inside you that is mine. You cannot be anything other than mine."

"I won't be like you," Bobbie promised. "You're selfish. I'm not going to be."

She stepped outside the protective circle.

Gran lunged at Bobbie and reached for her throat. But Jasper was quicker. He swung hard. The scarf lost all shape when the copper bell smacked into it. Cloth and metal writhed together like wounded snakes. Jasper dropped the whole mess and kicked it toward Rosa, who grabbed a handful of scarf, pulled, and stabbed.

Her sword punched through fabric.

A shriek tore the air, and then faded.

"Is she gone?" Humphrey asked. "Did you just kill our dead grandmother?"

Rosa caught her breath, lost it, and caught it again. "Nope," she finally said. "Can't be done. Already dead."

Tim jumped down to the floor, climbed over the motionless scarf, and kicked it several times until it caught fire. Jasper gently picked up the wraith and stomped the fire out.

"What do we do when she comes back?" Bobbie

asked. It wasn't a demand. Just an honest question.

"Make a memorial," Rosa said. "Give her some tulips and a small corner of the garden. Nothing else. Ever. She'll stay there. And then she'll stay away from your neck."

"The garden doesn't exist anymore," Humphrey pointed out.

"Make do with potted plants until you have a garden. Now shush and look around. Something's weird." She held her sword ready.

"What is it?" Bobbie asked.

Jasper caught on. "You're outside the circle. But chalky ghosts still aren't chasing you."

The door to the playground opened with a slow creak.

The four living kids stared at it. Cold air and snowflakes swirled over the threshold. Jasper held Tim close to shield him from the wind.

"The dead kids are holding it open," Humphrey said as he peered through the stone.

That's weird, Rosa thought.

"That's perfect," she said out loud. "Quick. Outside. Both of you."

"Aren't you coming with us?" Bobbie asked.

"Nope," Rosa said. "We still have appeasement stuff to sort out here."

"Can I keep the worry stone?" Humphrey asked.

"Sure," Rosa said. "Use it to keep an eye out for your grandmother."

He bolted for the door.

Bobbie stayed put, agitated. "Our family has done amazing things too, you know. We've done *important* things."

"So not all Talcotts are vicious grandmothers or kid-poisoners?" Rosa asked sweetly.

"No," Bobbie said.

Rosa stopped making fun of her. "Ancestry is like that. We don't get to choose. I wish we could. My dad died inventing a new kind of stupid."

"How?" Bobbie asked.

"Maybe I'll tell you later. Right now you need to be anywhere else. Try the library. Safest place to be if Gran comes back. Go."

Bobbie went.

The door remained open.

Jasper retrieved his bell and pulled it away from the torn, scorched scarf. "Talk to me, librarian."

"The chalk ghosts weren't chasing Talcotts," Rosa said. "I think they're trying to *protect* us. Maybe we should . . ."

Rosa stopped, stared, and dropped her sword.

Her father walked into the room.

🌿 28 🌿

"MR. LUCIUS?" JASPER ASKED.

The substitute history teacher leaned on his cane in a rakish and gentlemanly sort of way. He carried a leather briefcase in his other hand. "Jasper. Rosa. You shouldn't be here, either of you. School is closed for the day."

The door to the playground slammed shut as he spoke.

Rosa grabbed Jasper and yanked them both inside the chalk circle.

"Hey!" he said, caught off guard. Then he saw the stricken look on her face.

Mr. Lucius set down the briefcase, took off his

glasses, and tucked them into a shirt pocket. His posture shifted. Jasper recognized that kind of shift. It happened when performers stepped right out of character.

"Your little circle won't work very well against the living, Rosa," said the man who was not Mr. Lucius anymore.

"You're alive," she whispered. "You grew a beard. You've got glasses. And a cane. And a limp. And you're *alive*. I thought you were haunting me. I kept thinking that my history teacher looked a whole lot like my dad because my dad was *haunting* me. But I knew that you couldn't be him. Not really. Because my teacher's alive and you're dead. I thought you were dead."

Jasper's sense of the whole situation took a huge leap sideways. He set Tim on the floor, right in the center of the chalk circle, and kept him hidden behind his hand.

"Get help," he whispered. "Rosa pulled her sword through here. Go back the same way. Try not to set her room on fire when you get there."

The fiery ghost flickered once and then disappeared.

Rosa's father, Ferdinand Díaz, approached them slowly. His cane made echoing taps against the cafeteria floor. "I have your mother to thank for the limp. She stabbed my leg right before my library fell around us both. A gifted duelist, your mother." He sounded very proud.

Rosa felt utterly cold. The molten center of her world solidified and stopped moving. "I saw you die. I saw your library fall. And I saw you today. At the Talcott house. Right before that building came down, too. Buildings keep falling on you. And *nothing* survives inside a banishment circle. Not when it breaks. Not ever."

Her father smiled a sad and embarrassed sort of smile. "Letheans do. How could we improve our art if we extinguished ourselves every time anything went wrong?"

Rosa stepped out of her useless circle, pushed Jasper behind her, and picked up her sword. The edge had gashed the floor where she had dropped it.

Crap, she thought. *I damaged the cafeteria floor. With a sword. I brought a sword to school and scratched up the floor with it. Swords are bigger than pocketknives. Principal Ahmed is going to have some very angry words with me about this—or at least he will if he ever gets his voice back, the voice that he lost because Lethean things are scribbled all over the inside of the water fountain right next to the classroom where my father has been quizzing us about ancient Roman history for months.*

"Why did you steal all those voices?" In her head the words sounded like a formal challenge. In her own ears they were plaintive, like the cry of a wounded animal cub. *Why? Why? Why?*

"I only really meant to take *yours*, Rosa." He stood right outside the farthest reach of her sword. "Yours and Jasper's. The two of you undid the most splendid, shining, long-lasting banishment that the modern age has ever seen. I've spent most of my life studying Ingot. You made those studies much more difficult, my dear. So I needed to shut you up—temporarily—while I tracked down the ghost of Franz Talcott. But I missed you. I silenced many other people instead. Mea culpa. But all of that collateral damage did keep you busy, at least. And by keeping the voices away from their owners I have stoked more resentment between the living and the dead—which is as it should be."

Rosa held her sword higher and shifted her stance.

Her father watched with a critical eye. His voice became lower, slower, and more of a chant. "I see you have forgotten how to fight."

"No I haven't," Rosa insisted.

"Is that a strong position?"

"Yes," she said. "Yes, it is."

"Are you sure?"

She wasn't.

He twisted the handle of his cane and drew out a narrow blade. "How well do you remember swordsmanship? You seem so cute when you pretend to fight."

Rosa's muscle memories grew fuzzy. The weight of

the sword felt ungainly and uncertain to her. And then her father reached out with his own, caught the two blades in a bind, and took her weapon away, gently, as though confiscating a sharp pair of scissors from a very small child.

Rosa stared at her hand like she couldn't remember how it came to be empty.

Jasper grabbed that hand and pulled. "You know how to run!" he shouted at her, trying to break whatever spell her father's voice had cast. "You still remember how to run!"

They bolted for the exit, but the heavy door refused to open when they got there.

"Thresholds are mine," said Mr. Díaz in a kindly and apologetic sort of way. "Appeasement specialists tend to ask politely, but Letheans have more authority. Much more. That door will only remember how to open when I allow it."

Jasper gave up on kicking the door. "Help is coming," he whispered. "We just have to keep away from him until it gets here."

"Doesn't matter." Rosa's voice sounded just as cold, flat, and transparent as a new sheet of ice over a shallow pond. "Nobody else can get in. Not if every door and threshold only listens to him."

"She's right," her father called from the center of

the room. He hadn't bothered to chase after them. He knew that they had nowhere to go.

"'Keep fire and iron flowing through your blood,'" Jasper said quietly. "'Speak to danger in its language, or offer it your own. Understand yourself as dangerous.'"

"That's from *Dialogues of the Skill,*" said Rosa.

"Yes."

"You're quoting my patron librarian at me."

"Yes. Is it working?"

"Maybe."

"Good. Come on. Let's get somewhere out of reach." He took her hand and ran for the far corner of the cafeteria. Thick gym ropes dangled there.

Rosa looked up. "This is the worst possible escape plan. Those ropes don't go anywhere except the ceiling."

"Your dad is on the floor," Jasper said. "I'd rather be on the ceiling. All we have to do is stall."

"Help isn't coming," she said.

"'Make time by moving!'" he told her.

Ferdinand Díaz continued the quote. "'The quick create time itself by their motion.'"

Rosa and Jasper each grabbed a rope. Empty space opened up below them as they climbed.

"I loathe heights," she confessed.

"You're kidding," he said.

"Nope."

"But we climbed several dozen trees over the summer."

"I know," Rosa said. "It was terrifying. But I needed to prove that I could do it anyway."

"Of course you did," said Jasper. "Don't look down."

She looked down. The floor was already very far away. Her father stood on it, directly below. He looked worried about her.

"Are you sure that you remember how to climb?" he asked, his voice full of concern.

Rosa was no longer sure. Her hands slipped.

She fell.

29

ROSA'S FATHER DROPPED HIS CANE AND CAUGHT
her. The impact drove him down to one knee, but he
made sure that Rosa didn't hit the floor.

"I've got you," he said gently.

She felt safe. Then she didn't. All feelings of safety
died. He got her. He caught her. She was caught.

A patron medallion hung from a chain around his
neck, right beside her face. It showed a man wearing a
toga and standing in front of a very big wall. The inscription read, LUCIUS DOMITIUS AURELIANUS AUGUSTUS.

"Emperor Aurelian," she said.

"Yes," Dad said, clearly pleased.

"He burned down the Library of Alexandria."

Dad shook his head. "He helped the world free itself from the nightmares of our history. Think of it." He reached into his pocket and produced a clear vial of liquid. "Although I also need you to *stop* thinking about it, because I'm going to expel myself from your memory. It breaks my heart to do this. You will be happier afterward, however."

Jasper shouted something from the ceiling, but Rosa couldn't make out what he said.

"Stay where you are," Dad answered him. "I'd rather not kill you. I would also prefer not to permanently strip away every single memory that you have, excepting the memory of how to breathe. I only mean to confiscate a necessary few from you both."

Jasper started to climb down anyway. Rosa stopped him with a look. *Don't. Don't die. Don't you dare. I'll make sure that your memorial inscription says ridiculous things about you if you die.*

Her father opened the vial.

"What is that?" she asked him.

"Distilled amnesia," he said. "My own special recipe. You won't remember that I was ever here, that we ever spoke, or that I ever uttered these words. And your voice will be gone. I do promise to keep it safe, and to give it back as soon as I find what I'm looking for. I'll return all of the confiscated voices, and allow the school to reopen, just as soon as I have what I need. Then you'll be able to live your life and light small candles in vague remembrance of your dear, departed dad."

Rosa saw swirls and eddies of chalk dust in the air around them. Her father did not notice.

"Remember me fondly," he said. "Forget that I'm still alive. Forget that I'm close, so very close to learning how to banish the dead *permanently*. We'll be able to expel them from living memory. We'll make walled cities safe from every painful echo of our past, just as Aurelian restored Rome with the walls that he built."

The medallion caught the light with a coppery glint.

Rosa grabbed it and pulled. The chain broke.

"Now," she said to the ghosts who surrounded them. "You can touch him now."

Hands made of chalk dust pulled at her father's hair. He opened his mouth wide in surprise.

Rosa plucked the vial of distilled amnesia from his hand and poured it down his throat.

"Goodbye, Dad," she whispered. "I'm sorry that you won't remember this moment. But I always will."

After that, several things happened at once.

Jasper slid down the gym rope so fast he burned his hands from the friction.

Athena Díaz knocked the door down. She wore

heavy boots and a bathrobe. Her hair was wet and dusted with snow. In her right hand she held an Elizabethan broadsword, and in her left she carried a lantern with Tim blazing bright inside.

Chalk dust spun in a delighted whirlwind around Rosa's father, who sat down bewildered and stared at the floor.

Rosa's mother charged at him. "Get away from her!" she roared, broadsword held high.

"Shush," Rosa said to everyone, and then everyone was still—though Mom still looked like a river spirit intent on drowning absolutely everyone except for her own child.

"What happened?" she asked. "What did he do? Why is he breathing?"

"He's alive," Rosa told her. "And he's free of his own history now, so he got what he wanted. Sort of. Why are you in a bathrobe?"

"I was taking a shower," Mom said. "Your friend almost put himself out trying to get my attention." She held up the lantern. Tim waved. Rosa waved back. "That was alarming for everyone involved. Risky thing, setting a ghost made of fire running loose in a library. He left burn marks on the laundry scattered all over your bedroom floor."

"Oops," Jasper said. "Sorry."

"Don't be." Her voice was light, but her gaze was heavy. She watched Ferdinand Díaz and did not look away. "Please don't be."

Ghosts made chalky shapes and then scattered again. Hands tugged at Rosa and Jasper, beckoning.

Mom noticed. "You've got work to do."

"I don't want to leave you alone with him," Rosa told her.

"Go. I'll mind your father." She loomed over him and peered at his face in the flickering Tim-light. "Don't worry about us. This is the same blade that I used to outmatch him the last time he tried to pick a fight. But I don't think he's going to pick any fights now."

Rosa didn't think so either. Her father seemed peaceful, content, and barely there. "What's going to happen to him?"

"We'll give him to the archivists," Mom said, and that was all that she would say about it. "Now get to work, both of you. This place is itching with unfinished business. You're the specialists here. Finish it."

"Okay." Rosa kissed the top of her mother's head, which tasted like shampoo.

Jasper opened the briefcase that Rosa's dad had left beside the door. Rows of tiny glass vials rested inside. Each one contained a smoky liquid and was labeled with a name.

"Tracey, Mike, Chetna, River, Genevieve, Lex . . . these are voices, all of the stolen voices. Including the ones he took today. We can give them all back!"

Students made out of chalk took shape around the briefcase.

"I think someone else needs to borrow them first," Rosa said.

They took the voices to the haunted water fountain. Rosa used an old coin to scratch the Lethean inscriptions off of all the plumbing. Jasper turned the knob inside to restore the flow of water.

Chalky figures watched them work.

Rosa felt relieved to be working.

"You okay there, librarian?" Jasper asked her.

"Don't ask," she said. "If we just keep busy then I won't have to find out."

She put the access panel back into place. He tore away the OUT OF ORDER sign. Both of them turned to address the surrounding ghosts.

"You may *borrow* these voices," Rosa said. "But tomorrow you have to return them. Agreed?"

Each ghostly student raised a hand.

"Good."

Rosa and Jasper emptied the vials into the fountain, one at a time.

"Are you sure this is going to work?" Jasper whispered. He held the one marked TRACEY, which he really didn't want to pour down the drain.

"I'm never completely sure of anything," Rosa admitted. "But I think so. Maybe? Probably."

"Sometimes I wish you'd pretend to be sure," Jasper said. He poured out Tracey's voice. "Okay. That's all of them."

The ghosts lined up in front of the fountain. They took turns, and took sips. The water made it difficult to hold their chalky shapes together.

"They need more raw material," Rosa said. She went into the classroom and clapped erasers. Clouds of chalk dust that used to be written words billowed across the room. Chalky students took shape behind every desk.

One boy stood apart from the others. When he spoke he sounded just like Principal Ahmed. "They need you to know their names. No one else remembers their names."

"Tell us," said Rosa.

The students tried to speak all at once, but it came out in a jumbled chorus of whispers.

"Write them," Jasper suggested.

One ghost stood up from her desk, walked to the chalkboard, and wrote her name in cursive script with the tip of one finger. The rest followed. They took turns. Some spit dust at the board in the shapes of their names. Others smacked the slate until it took on their names. Some passed right through the chalkboard and returned, leaving their names behind them.

Rosa wrote every one on the back of a history quiz.

"We'll take attendance from now on," she promised. "Every morning a living teacher will name you, here in this room. We won't forget."

"Thank you," said the boy who stood apart.

"What's *your* name?" Jasper asked him, though he had suspicions already.

"Franz Talcott," he said. "The first mayor of Ingot. I already wrote it. I tried to tell you who I was."

"You seem younger now than you were when you died." Jasper said.

"Yes. At this age I believe that I was at my best."

"Probably true," Rosa said. "As a grown-up you poisoned every other ghost in this room."

"Yes," he said simply. "It was an accident."

"And after that you banished them all."

"Then I died," Franz Talcott said. "The boss banished me along with all the rest."

"Now they protect you," said Rosa. "They made the circle around the Lump to keep prying Letheans like my father away from you."

"They did," said the ghost. "They sing old circle games to make a ring of safety around my haunted place. Ashes, ashes, a ring around the roses."

"I would have been less forgiving," Rosa said.

Jasper cleared his throat in a very obvious attempt to say *Stop that. We're supposed to settle old grudges, not rile them up.*

Fine, she said in the way that she crossed her arms.

"What do *you* need?" Rosa asked out loud. "What sort of memorial does the first mayor of Ingot require?"

"None," he told her. "I have the tree, and the hill, and the well that I made. Nothing else should be remembered as mine."

"Agreed," Rosa said, but then her voice softened. "My dad can't find you there. Not now. He can't seek out your secrets or use them to hurt anyone else. Thanks. To all of you. I'd be voiceless right now without your help."

Franz Talcott nodded once before he faded away.

The other chalky figures collapsed at their desks.

Outside, in the playground, the circle that surrounded the Lump broke apart. Fallen ice and frozen leaves took on the shapes of children. They held hands to make a ring and processed in a slow circle, singing to themselves.

The song ended.

They all fell down.

School opened again on the following day.

Everyone squeezed into the hallway outside the history classroom. All of the silenced students and teachers lined up at the water fountain. Tracey, Mike, Chetna, River, Genevieve, Lex, and Principal Ahmed had been bereft of their voices for weeks, so the seven of them stood at the front of the line.

"Just drink," Rosa told them. "That's all you have to do."

"The ghosts of this place didn't take your voices away," Jasper added, "but they did help us find them. Now they're going to give them back."

Maybe, Rosa thought, but managed not to say.

Gladys-Marie stood right nearby and watched her twin with a fierce, fragile hope that was painful to see. Rosa looked away. She locked eyes with Bobbie Talcott, who wore a new, loose scarf to cover dark bruises. But this scarf did not twitch, make itself into fingers, or make new bruises over the old. Those potted tulips were working so far. Nell was hard at work making a memorial plaque, which should be done by the end of the day. Gran would get her due, and nothing else.

Bobbie nodded to Rosa. Rosa nodded back. She

didn't know if that exchange of nods meant that they were friends now, or enemies bound by new and mutual respect. She felt good about it either way.

The principal was brave enough to take the first sip from the haunted fountain.

Jasper held his breath. Rosa bounced up and down on her toes a few times.

Mr. Ahmed straightened up and cleared his throat. "Welcome, students, to a new day at school. This is your principal speaking."

Everyone who could speak cheered wildly.

Tracey went next. She drank, said a tentative hello to her twin sister, and then knocked Rosa right over with a tackling hug.

DECEMBER

✺ 30 ✺

IT WAS DAWN ON THE MORNING OF THE WINTER
solstice. Tonight would be the longest night of the year.
After that the days would lengthen and slowly remember what sunlight was like.

A procession wound through Ingot in the early
morning light.

They carried lanterns. Most had made simple,
temporary lamps out of paper and wire, or cardboard
and cellophane, but a few used sturdy metal frames
and glass panels to protect their candles from wind and
snow.

The cold caused some grumbling. The whole procession wore medieval and renaissance garb made for

summer festivals, not winter weather. A few townsfolk
had wrapped blankets over their costumes. Others gave
up on historical authenticity and zipped ski jackets over
finery. The rest braved the cold and shivered in their
archaic clothes. But they all marched together, despite
the weather and their own apprehension about the place
that they were marching toward.

Her majesty the queen of the Ingot Renaissance
Festival led the procession on horseback. Her champion
rode beside her in full and resplendent armor.

Jasper followed both of his parents on foot. He carried his quarterstaff in one hand and the refinery bell in
the other. He felt reasonably warm, with long underwear
underneath his squire outfit. He also felt horribly nervous
about the whole march. It had been his idea. But the idea
had its own momentum now that it was out of his head and
moving through the world. Hundreds of footsteps carried
it forward. Jasper couldn't have stopped it if he tried.

Rosa did not feel nervous. She wore the improvised
costume of a sixteenth-century Spanish traveler and
whistled while she marched. Her ornate metal lantern
held a dancing Tim.

Sir Dad leaned over to speak with her. "Thank you
for your part in this, Lady Rosa."

"Good sir," Rosa said, "I am Catalina de Erauso,
and no lady at all."

Sir Dad grinned. He loved it when people stayed in character. "I do beg your pardon."

"You have my pardon," Rosa told him. "But I shouldn't have your thanks. My part has been small. This was all your squire's plan. And you probably shouldn't thank him, either, until after we know that it's going to work out."

Jasper kicked the heel of Rosa's boot. She kicked him back.

"I respectfully disagree," said Sir Dad. "This is a fine thing to take part in, regardless of the outcome."

"Oh. Okay. You're welcome, then." Rosa was surprised to notice just how happy that made her feel. *We broke your festival*, she thought. *Maybe now we can fix it. All of us.*

"Your father isn't a terrible person," she whispered. "That's nice."

"It is," Jasper agreed. "Any news about yours?"

"Nope," said Rosa. "Archivists aren't very talkative. I don't know how he's doing, or what he remembers. But I know that they've got him. He's there. He isn't here. That's enough." She lowered her voice, a little embarrassed. "I don't mind knowing that he was good at his craft—even though the things that he did with it were awful. That's strangely comforting. I don't know why. Maybe because we feel more alike now? I want to be good at what I do. The best. But I don't want to be like him. And now I feel more solidly sure that I'll never grow up to be like him. Never, ever, ever, in a thousand years of Thursdays. I'm also glad that he's still alive."

Some of the townsfolk struck up a marching tune. Rosa swung her lantern to the same beat, which Tim seemed to enjoy. "And I'm glad to be dressed up as my hero and wearing a sword out in public. Not *my* sword. That would be historically inaccurate by a thousand years. But Nell let me borrow something more period-specific. I like it. Maybe she'll let me keep it."

Nell made a noise of gruff bemusement behind them. "Only after years of free labor will I let you keep that sword."

"Okay," Rosa agreed. "I've been meaning to visit Tim more often anyway." The fire wraith bowed inside his lantern. He was much happier in Nell's forge than he had been in his library haunts.

Athena Díaz made a thoughtful and skeptical noise. She wore a long, flowing gown somewhere under a very thick blanket. "Are you sure about taking on extra work? School appeasements still keep you busy."

"I'll manage," Rosa promised. "The school has calmed down lately. And now we've got The Thing from Behind the Cafeteria Refrigerator patrolling at night. That helps." She savored the weight of the sword at her side. "Hey, does our school have a fencing team?"

"No," Jasper said. "It really should, though, given the number of festival folk in this town."

"Let's start one."

"Sure. But one thing at a time."

Rosa poked him with her elbow. "You're nervous."

"And you have become more skilled at noticing very obvious things about the living." He expected them to swap insults back and forth for a bit, but Rosa didn't take up his challenge.

"This is going to work," she said.

"Are you sure?"

"Nope. It *might* work. Maybe. Possibly. Probably. But no matter what happens I can promise that it's going to be fun."

"Two entire armies of ghosts might attack us," Jasper pointed out.

"I know!" Rosa loosened her sword in its sheath. "Fun."

The procession left the roads and sidewalks of Ingot. They crossed over fields and came to a halt at the festival gates.

Jasper told his parents to dismount. "We'll have to leave the living horses out here. They might freak out inside."

"*We* might freak out inside," Nell said.

Rosa's mother stepped on Nell's foot.

Sir Dad and Queen Mom hitched their horses. Jasper opened the padlocked gates with the approximate birth year of Geoffrey of Monmouth. Then he threw a pebble at the ground.

The cold stones that were Jerónimo pulled together through frozen dirt.

Both living horses whinnied unhappily. Murmurs of alarm spread through the gathered townsfolk. Some people turned around and marched right home at the sight.

"The freaking out has begun . . . ," Rosa said.

"Good practice for what they're about to see inside," said Jasper. "And I need Ronnie for this. I need to be noticed. None of this will work if I can't command attention."

"You hate attention."

"True. Hold all of this stuff for a second?"

She took the staff and bell while he mounted up.

Jasper could see every face in the crowd from astride his haunted horse. Doris the fortune-teller watched him hopefully. Odds Bodkin whispered something to Duncan Barnstaple. Most of the acrobats from the Human Dice Game were here, and so were the mermaids who were sometimes piratical warrior maids. Every member of Zwerchhau Whirligig had come home for this, and brought trumpets.

Almost half of Ingot stood in that snowy field. They all fixed their gaze on Jasper. He took a breath. Then he took the staff and bell back from Rosa. A nudge with his knees steered Ronnie through the gates.

Ghostly figures made of leaves and snow gathered around the far edges of the market square. They watched the procession in absolute silence.

The day's battle had not yet begun, but both ghostly armies had already lined up on opposite sides of the jousting grounds.

Jasper led the procession onto the field between them. Zwerchhau Whirligig announced the arrival of the living with trumpeted fanfare.

The scarecrow army stirred at the sound. The scarecrow queen and her champion rode forward on horses made of wood and cloth. Both the riders and their steeds moved as though dangerous and solid, despite their flimsy raw material. Sir Morien bore a new shield sculpted out of ice.

A squire followed behind them on foot. He carried the tattered remains of a royal banner. Jasper was surprised to see a patched-together version of himself. *Didn't think that I'd played the character memorably enough to leave any lasting echoes behind. I guess this is a good sign.*

Sir Morien drew his sword, and so did Sir Dad.

That's not such a good sign.

Jasper quickly spurred Ronnie between them. He was not merely a squire today, but a messenger, and he pitched his voice to carry far.

"Your grace," he said, addressing both versions of the queen. "This place is yours in summer. It will always be yours in summer, and in summertime the living will return to bring life and breath back into our shared roles. The festival will live again. But this place is yours in no other time or season."

The two monarchs regarded each other.

"Agreed," said Queen Mom.

Her scarecrow self nodded once, and then collapsed.

Sir Morien raised his sword to salute Sir Dad. Then he fell apart.

All of the festival ghosts became random pieces of wreckage and debris.

The living procession took their place.

"That went well," Rosa said cheerfully.

"That was the easy part," Jasper reminded her. "I figured the scarecrows would probably listen to us. They *are* us. We made them. The other crowd of ghosts is older and angrier."

"But you do have something that they'll listen to," she said. "Probably."

Jasper nudged Ronnie forward, toward the gathered company of the mining dead. They hoisted their pickaxes, clearly itching for their daily battle. Blinding headlamps all focused on Jasper. He squinted and blinked in the glare.

The miners came forward, a roiling crowd eager to break things.

Jasper struck the refinery bell with his quarterstaff. It rang clear and clean in the winter air. The sound had marked every break and the end of every workday at the old refinery. It meant *stop*.

The ghostly army stopped, and they listened, though they did not set down their arms.

"This place is yours in winter!" Jasper called out. "This is your home. Welcome home. Be always welcome here. Recognize it. Cease your search. Treat the theater stage as your town meeting hall, and hold midwinter dances undisturbed by the living. This place is yours in winter. Claim it. But understand that the fairgrounds belong to you in no other time or season. Stand aside and find your rest when summer comes."

Nothing happened. No one moved. Jasper waited for some kind of answer, still squinting in the glare of so many headlamps.

The miners moved closer. Jasper's hand tightened on the leather-wrapped grip of his quarterstaff, prepared to fend off pickaxes and shovels. But those tools dissolved into powdered stone. Their work was done. The bell had sounded.

Ghosts removed caps and helmets, ending their searchlight glare.

Jasper tried to keep calm while he led the procession away, but two words shouted inside his head: *It worked, it worked, it worked, it worked, it worked!*

Most of the living set their lanterns on the ground. Lost wisps filled the air and found warmth and welcome in each candle flame. Two poltergeists juggled snowballs. Larger, stranger things came down from the mountains. The procession processed more quickly to keep well clear of their lumbering way.

Piano music sounded from the Mousetrap Stage. Franz Talcott, still a child, played ice-sculpted keys. More and more ghosts made shapes for themselves out of falling snow. They began to dance.

The living departed through the open gates, yielding the fairgrounds to the dead of winter.

Rosa swung her Tim-lit lantern, skipped a quick dance step, and whistled along with the music.

ACKNOWLEDGMENTS

My thanks to Alice Dodge, Kekla Magoon, M. T. Anderson, Peter S. Beagle, Karen Meisner, Amy Rose Capetta, Cori McCarthy, Nova Ren Suma, David Macinnis Gill, Cynthia Leitich Smith, Susan Fletcher, Anne Ursu, Laura Ruby, Nicole Griffin, Colleen A.F. Venable, Rio Saito, Leah Schwartz, Kasey Princell, Ellen Oh, Lucy Bellwood, Ivan Bialostosky, and Nathan Clough for their knowledge, wisdom, inspiration, friendship, and support.

More thanks to Barry Goldblatt, Tricia Ready, Nicole Fiorica, Karen Wojtyla, and Kelly Murphy for their endless professional excellence.

Raise a glass.